BOOKS BY SCOTT CORBETT

Witch

Hunt

Witch

Hunt

by
Scott Corbett

Joy Street Books
Little, Brown and Company
BOSTON   TORONTO

SECOND PRINTING

Library of Congress Cataloging-in-Publication Data

Corbett, Scott.
  Witch hunt.
"A Joy Street book."

  Summary: Sixteen-year-old Les and his best friend
get involved in a murder case when they stumble across
a coven of witches plotting revenge against a
troublesome lawyer.
  [1. Witchcraft—Fiction.   2. Mystery and detective
stories] I. Title.
PZ.C79938Wi 1985   [Fic]   85-47783
ISBN 0-316-15750-3

RRD

Published simultaneously in Canada

PRINTED IN THE UNITED STATES OF AMERICA

To Judge William M. Mackenzie,

whom many a murderer

learned to respect

Witch

Hunt

1

ONE THING WALLY BRENNER and I shared was a taste for crime detection. It was a taste we developed in the Canby House case, after Mr. Canby's death, when his house was moved to Adamsport Village.

Wally's uncle, Matt Brenner, was Adamsport's chief of police. For our brilliant work on that case we got a brief thank-you followed by "— but I want to tell you, if ever I catch you sticking your noses into police matters again, you're going to wish you'd never —"

He went on to list several things we'd wish we'd never, none of them pleasant.

So from then on we had no intention of stepping out of line. Absolutely no intention. But you know how it is. . . .

* * *

We had the day off from our jobs at the Village. We'd planned to do some yard work for our regular customers, but the Brenners' postman changed all that. He dropped the mail through the front door slot just as I swung into the driveway and parked my Yamakura motorbike.

When I came through the back door into the kitchen, it was about nine-thirty. Wally and his mother were still sitting at the breakfast table in the sunny bay window, and his father, J.G., was coming back from the front hall with the mail.

"Morning, Lester, you're just in time. Here it is, the latest poop from everybody's favorite shyster, Leonard Billings. That man's in the right profession — I never saw anyone who loved to put people's backs up more than he does — a more contentious man never lived — he counts it a day lost when he isn't mucking around with someone's property, trying to do them out of —"

"Now, how can you be so sure?" Mrs. Brenner wanted to know. "You haven't even read his letter yet."

"I don't have to. I confidently predict that this letter will have to do with that woodlot of ours over in Compton, next to Minnie Crowell's, and I further predict that Lawyer Billings will claim

4

his client owns a strip of our lot — just like he found *he* owned Fletcher's Knoll instead of Standish Thornton, right when Standish and his coven of witches were really beginning to enjoy it. I'll bet they're planning to put a heavy hex on Leonard for that one, and I may have to join them. Do you suppose Standish would welcome an assistant warlock?"

The Thorntons, Standish and his sister Hester, were the last remnants of one of our oldest families. They had always been a bit eccentric, but lately they'd gotten worse. Rumor had it they were deeply involved in witchcraft. They were convinced they possessed occult powers inherited from various shadowy ancestors who went all the way back to the witchcraft scares of Puritan times.

"Well, anyway, let's see what Lawyer Billings has to say this time," said J.G., and opened the letter. " 'Billings and Gould, Attorneys at Law, Turk's Head Building —' "

"We know the address."

"Quiet, dear. I want you to get the whole pompous flavor of this. 'Dear Mr. —' "

J.G. stopped short. He glanced at the envelope — "No, it's addressed to me!" — and went back to the letter.

5

" 'Mr. Standish Thornton, Thornton Farm, Queen Anne's Road' — and so forth — 'Dear Mr. Thornton . . .' "

"J.G.! Now, hold on, there's clearly a mix-up here, and I don't hold with reading other people's mail!"

J.G. promptly folded up the letter.

"You're right. Far be it from me to intrude on another person's sacred privacy. I'm sure it's a mighty interesting letter — the little bit that *did* slip past my eyes certainly was — but I promise to keep it strictly to myself."

For a moment he silently enjoyed the spectacle of his glaring, squirming wife, then took off again.

"Yes, you're absolutely right, my pet — there's some mix-up here, and we shouldn't read it. But on the other hand, it's too late. We're all going to die of curiosity now if we don't know what it says. So here goes: 'Dear Mr. Thornton: if you and your so-called coven of witches trespass *once more* upon that portion of my property known as Fletcher's Knoll, I shall take appropriate steps to make sure it does not happen again. Sincerely yours, Leonard Billings.' Well, sir! For a lawyer, that's a pretty straightforward letter. Blunt, you might even call it. Our resident warlock is not going to be happy about *this!*"

"Not to mention having someone else read it first!"

"Well, if I got his, maybe he got mine."

J.G. was reaching for the kitchen phone when it rang.

"Witches? . . . Hello?" He nodded at us. "Hi, Standish. . . . You did? Well — Yes, I did," said J.G., then winced and held the phone away from his ear.

As usual, Wally Brenner was thinking fast, scheming.

"Tell him we'll bring it right out to them, Dad!"

"Now, hold on, Standish, it's . . . I know, but . . . Yes, I agree, Leonard Billings leaves a lot to be desired, but — Listen, Standish, my son Wally and Les Cunningham are here, they'll bring it out right away. Be there in five minutes! Yes! Okay, Standish — good-bye!"

J.G. hung up and massaged his ear.

"Wow! If anybody wants a wild warlock, we have one in stock! That man is *mad!* In all senses of the word, maybe! I'm glad you piped up, Wally, it helped me get him off the line."

"Listen, Dad, I wouldn't miss the chance to get inside that house and see him and his sister when they're really winging it!"

7

J.G. picked up the phone again, glanced at the letter, and dialed.

"I'm going to — Good morning! This is J. G. Brenner. I'd like to speak to Leonard Billings. What? His line's busy? I'll bet it is!" cackled J.G. "Never mind, I'll call again later."

He hung up and grinned at us.

"I guess Standish beat me to the draw. That girl sounded pretty flustered. Get going, boys — and I want a full report, Wally. I'll be going over to the store shortly, so call me there."

Mrs. Brenner glanced at them both.

"Like father, like son," she said gloomily. "One just as nosy as the other!"

2

M RS. BRENNER WAS RIGHT ON
all counts. Wally was a compact bundle of live
wires with enough curiosity programmed into his
system to stock nine generations of cats. We made
a funny-looking pair, I suppose, he short and solid,
I built like a stork on a diet, all legs and arms.
In many ways we were such a study in contrasts
I'm surprised we were friends. We couldn't even
walk down the street together without problems.
Wally's idea of walking was something just this
side of breaking into a run; I liked to amble. Our
eating habits didn't jibe, either. He bolted his food;
I liked to take my time. I said he made sea gulls
look dainty; he said I made cows look intelligent.

Nine years ago I'd been an upright, straightforward, trustworthy seven-year-old. Then we

moved to Adamsport and I landed in a second-grade class with Wally, and since then I've become almost as much of a schemer and conniver as he is, out of self-defense!

And I'll admit I was every bit as curious as he was about Thornton Farm. I was ready when he said, "If we take Linden Street, that'll get us to Queen Anne's Road the quickest!"

Speaking of cats, one leaped for his life in front of us.

"See that black cat cross our path?" I asked at a stoplight. "Not what you want when you're going to visit witches!"

Another of our differences. I tended to be mildly superstitious, but Wally was snooty-scientific. I'd ask him, "What's wrong with a few superstitions? They don't cost anything, and they might save your life!" That always set him off.

Thornton Farm was two or three miles out of town, out where houses were few and far between, with lots of acreage. For the most part, people like Leonard Billings lived out there, not to mention his partner, Ronald Gould. We soon spotted a black mailbox with "Thornton Farm" painted on it, and turned between two boulders into the weedy driveway. It curved around for a quarter of a mile before we came to the house.

10

It was a beaut: a colonial farmhouse with three or four additions to the original house. Paint was peeling from the woodwork; the weathered gray shingles needed attention. A dozen enormous trees drooped around it on all sides. If there had once been a lawn under them, it was now underbrush that could have hidden tigers. At that time of year, late in August, the trees' leaves kept every bit of morning sunshine off the place. If I'd been a house-hunting witch, I'd have bought it in a minute. Even the car parked in the driveway added to the effect, because it was at least fifteen years old, old and drab; a good make built to last.

Even though I've got the long legs, it was all I could do to keep on Wally's heels as he bustled up to the front door. There wasn't any doorbell button, but there was an old-fashioned wire bell-pull. He tried it. The result was an ear-splitting jangle that made us both jump. We backed off and waited. We heard shuffling footsteps inside. The door opened. It creaked and groaned like something straight out of a horror movie, and then a flurry of black rags with glittering black eyes backed us off another step. We had never seen Hester Thornton before, but we sure saw her now. She glared at us and all but screeched, "Are you the lads with the letter?"

It takes a lot to stop Wally, though, when he has a goal in mind, and his goal was to get inside that house and have a good look at everything, including both Thorntons.

"Yes, ma'am! We've brought the letter, and come to get my dad's," he said, and hustled in past her before she knew what was happening. And I was right on his heels. Wally looked around and said brightly, "Can we see Mr. Thornton?"

Hester drew herself up to an impressive height. She was a tall woman whose black ragbag of a dress, long and droopy, made her look even taller.

"My brother is waiting for you," she said in tones of doom. "Come this way."

She led us down a long narrow hallway papered with an ancient geometric pattern and into a small room where almost everything, including the paint on the walls, seemed to be a dull red. Seated in a tall black wooden armchair the size of a throne, carved within an inch of its life, was Standish Thornton.

We had seen *him* before, around town, but never looking like this. He had black hair, but now it was shiny black, and came down to a peak in the middle of his forehead. His sharp features — long nose, thin lips — looked even sharper now than I remembered them. He was wearing a black robe with big sleeves that hung down almost to the floor. His arms were stretched along the armrests, his fingers wrapped around the curved ends like claws. He was a picture of badly controlled, almost maniacal fury. He didn't bother to say hello. When he saw the letter Wally had taken out of his pocket, he simply stretched out one quivering hand.

Now, up to that point I may have been a little bug-eyed, but I was still telling myself that this whole scene, all this hocus-pocus, was a lot of nonsense. But then, just for a moment, my eyes sort of blurred, and the air was suddenly so stifling I could hardly breathe. Stifling, yet cold, icy cold. All my protective layers of modern-day thinking dropped away. I was scared.

Wally gave Standish the letter. Thornton took it out of the envelope, read it, and slowly crushed it in his fist. His voice, when he choked out a few words, sounded like something coming from underground.

"He'll pay for this. He's gone too far. He'll find out what kind of power he's trifling with! . . ."

"In our own way, Standish," murmured his sister. "In our own way, and in our own time."

Standish pointed to a table.

"Give them their letter."

13

Hester handed it to Wally. And with that, even he couldn't think of an excuse to hang around any longer. We had not exactly been invited to stay for coffee and Danish.

"Thank you," said Wally. "We're sorry about this."

Standish Thornton's dark eyes flamed at him. "*You* have nothing to be sorry about. Others do have — and *will* have."

"Come." His sister beckoned to us in an imperious way, and returned to the hallway. We followed meekly. She opened the creaking front door, stood aside with stony face, watched us go past, then creaked the door shut with a bang. We headed for our bikes.

"Gee, you're welcome," muttered Wally. "How do you like that? Not so much as a thank-you."

"Nicest folks you'd ever want to know," I agreed.

"But worth the trip!"

"I wouldn't have missed it. But I want to tell you, for a minute there I got a funny feeling —"

"Hold it. Let's talk later."

We had left gloom and doom about a mile behind us before Wally pulled off the road. Time for a conference.

"What about a funny feeling?"

14

"Did you get one, too? Hard to breathe, and cold?"

"Yes. If that was air-conditioning, they've got the fastest-working system I know of. But don't let your imagination run away with you! I think his stagecraft is better than his witchcraft. Pretty darn good, in fact. Got to us psychologically."

I had to goad him a little.

"In other words, what you're saying is, you don't think that sudden icy cold meant that a ghost or the Devil himself was on the scene, like some people claim."

"Now, listen —!"

"Never mind, we can talk about that later. I wonder who mixed up those letters? Laura Cervik would know, and I'll bet she's phoned all the news home to Mary by now. What say we start our yard work there?"

"*Now* you're making sense," said Wally. "Let's go!"

Laura Cervik and her sister were among our oldest customers. We'd been taking care of their yard ever since we started in the business five years ago. They lived in a small, neat cottage with a nice level lawn around it, hydrangea bushes on each side of the front door, and a few medium-sized trees scattered about. Miss Mary took care of the house, and Miss Laura worked — for the past twenty-five years or so at Billings & Gould.

When we reached the Cerviks' place, the first surprise was that Miss Mary wasn't out on such a fine morning grubbing in her flower beds. The second surprise came when the back door opened and it wasn't Mary who opened it, but Laura. Her usually bright plump face was woebegone. She looked as if she'd been crying.

"Miss Laura! How come you're home?"

"Oh, Wally! Your father got the wrong letter, didn't he?"

"Yes, he did. We just took it to Mr. Thornton."

"Oh, this is terrible! Terrible! Come in, I want to hear all about it! What did your father say? How did Mr. Thornton take it?"

Inside we found Miss Mary sitting at the table in their breakfast nook. She was a tiny woman who looked gentle and frail — a total illusion, for she was the hardheaded, practical member of the family. She waved a hand in the direction of a plateful of the world's best homemade cinnamon buns, and we knew we were about to make up for the Danish and coffee we didn't get at our last stop.

"Sit down, boys. Maybe you can help me talk some sense into Laura," she added as she put plates and cups in front of us. "She's making a mountain out of a molehill."

"I am *not!*" Laura glared at her sister, thumped herself down onto a chair, and turned to us for support. "Why *shouldn't* I be upset? Mr. Billings dictated those letters to me, and I typed them up and put them in their envelopes, so he blamed *me* for the mistake! I was so — so — well, I'm afraid I almost had hysterics. I must say, Mr. Gould was very kind, certainly a lot nicer than Mr. *Billings* was! Mr. Gould said I should go home for the rest of the day, and not to worry, and he even walked me down to my car. But I just can't believe it! How could I put those letters in the wrong envelopes? I'll tell you, I can't help having my suspicions. . . ."

Miss Mary glanced at us and rolled her eyes, but didn't interrupt.

"Now, this is just between us, and I know I can trust you boys, but — well, office politics can be a terrible thing, and I can tell you there's a certain person who'd like to step into my shoes as — well, sort of head secretary, I suppose you'd call it. I know for a fact she's said more than once it's time some old fuddy-duddies retire!"

"Who's 'she,' Miss Laura?"

"She's Cynthia McGinnis, a little snip in her twenties, with a cute shape and all that, and does she know it! Things haven't been the same since she came into the picture. For one thing, there's obviously something going on between her and Mr. Billings — though heaven knows he's always got some girl on the string. His poor wife, she's put up with plenty! Right now she's gone to visit her family in Maine for a month, so maybe she's thinking of a separation — but she'll never divorce him, that I know. And a divorce is the last thing *he'd* want, anyway, whatever a little fool like Cynthia may think. But, anyway —"

"Now, Laura, don't be silly," said Miss Mary. "Nobody opened those letters and switched them around!"

"Why not? They were in the Out basket on Cynthia's desk, right where anybody could get at them! I put them there just before it was time for Mr. Billings's coffee. He usually wants a cup around midmorning, so unless he says he doesn't I always go to the little pantry we have and bring him one. Then I fill Mr. Gould's electric pot with water and take it to his office, because he likes to heat the water and make his own tea right there,"

Laura said in an uncomplaining tone of voice. It was easy to see she loved a familiar routine, enjoyed being depended on for little things as well as important matters.

"But, Laura," said Miss Mary, "those letters were only in that basket for about half an hour before the postman came and picked them up. Why would anyone take the risk of doing such a silly thing, and how would they do it, anyway? Just for once you've got to face the fact that you *might* have made a mistake, and that it's not the end of the world if you did. Nobody's perfect!"

Laura struggled up out of her chair, which was a tight fit.

"Mary, you are being deliberately insulting!" she cried, and flounced out of the room. Her sister took all this completely in stride. When we were alone, she glanced at us and shook her head.

"Poor dear, she can't face the fact that maybe she *should* retire." Miss Mary leaned our way and dropped her voice. "Listen, do us a favor. She was so upset she forgot to bring home the one thing that might calm down her nerves —"

"Her knitting!"

We both came up with that answer, because we both owned sweaters she'd knitted for us. Miss

Laura Cervik was the all-time compulsive knitter.

"That's right. And she left it at the office. In the bottom right-hand drawer of her desk. Now, I was wondering —"

"We're on our way!"

3

WE WERE NOT ONLY DOING Miss Mary a favor, we were doing one for ourselves. Neither of us wanted to sit around much longer listening to Miss Laura moan and groan.

Adamsport is not a large town. Its business district is about six square blocks, and the tallest building is seven stories high. That's the Turk's Head Building, where Billings & Gould have their offices on the fifth floor. *All* of the fifth floor. The biggest law firm in town, not to mention the county.

We had parked our bikes and were heading up Main Street toward the Turk's Head when an old car went past that caught my eye.

"Hey! Look who's here! Wasn't that —?"

Wally hadn't missed it.

"Sure enough! Was he wearing his black robe?"

"I don't think so, but — What do you suppose he's up to?"

"Same thing as everybody else — looking for a parking space!"

"No, I mean —"

"Well, if he's got any ideas of paying a visit to Billings and Gould, I want a front seat! Come on — on the double!"

When we stepped out of the elevator on the fifth floor, ahead of us were double doors with "Billings & Gould, Attorneys at Law" and a string of lawyers' names on them. We each pulled open a door and walked in. Sitting behind a large desk, crooning "Billings and Goo-wuld, may I help you?" into a phone, was Cynthia the receptionist. Once she had transferred the call, she glanced up at us and said, "Yes?"

"Are you Miss McGinnis?"

She nodded.

"We've come to pick up Miss Laura's knitting. It's in her right-hand —"

"I know where she keeps it," said Cynthia, with a little smirk twitching at the corners of her lipstick. She told us to wait, and her high heels clicked away down a corridor to our left. In a moment she was back, carrying a bundle of knitting with big wooden needles stuck in it. She was about to hand it over, when the double doors were banged open.

Standish Thornton had changed his clothes, but he looked just as furious as he had the last time we'd seen him. I don't think he even took any of us in as he swept past.

"Sir! Just a minute!" cried Cynthia, but she might as well have been talking to a tidal wave. She rushed after him, and so did we. By the time we rounded the corner into a large room full of desks with people working at them, Standish had crossed it and was yanking open one of the private office doors. We heard a deep voice say, "What the —!" while Standish screamed, "You're not fit to live!" And then all hell broke loose.

Two or three of the younger lawyers jumped up and made a grab for him. He sent two of them flying, one of whom went sliding across a desktop. Several secretaries screamed. Mr. Billings, a large man but a trifle pudgy, came charging out of his office and tackled Standish along with a couple of reinforcements. Mr. Gould appeared, took a cool look at the situation, and with a quick move got the first effective hold on Standish. Another moment or two, and the thrashing warlock was finally overpowered, with about four lawyers on top of him.

23

"Somebody call the police!" bellowed Leonard Billings. By then, looking as calm as ever, Mr. Gould was already doing so. The battle had left him unmarked, but not so Mr. Billings. Somewhere along the line he had picked up a split lip, and he was patting it indignantly with his handkerchief. We stuck around, of course, until the police arrived — two patrolmen and Lieutenant Slade.

"Well, Lieutenant, I hope our good chief of police will take this maniac seriously now!" Lawyer Billings thundered in his best courtroom manner. Slade rolled his eyes and nodded.

"I hope so, too, sir!"

We didn't care for Lieutenant Slade's tone of voice. We knew all about Lieutenant Slade. He was a pushy young guy who considered himself the wave of the future, and plainly felt Uncle Matt was a nice old relic who simply wasn't with it anymore. He quickly and expertly snapped handcuffs into place, and his men pulled Standish to his feet. Standish glared savagely at Mr. Billings, then turned on Mr. Gould.

"I won't forget this!" he snarled.

Mr. Gould never turned a hair.

"I'm sorry, Standish, but what would you expect me to do?"

He asked the question in an almost detached and impersonal way, as if he were only mildly interested in the answer. He didn't get any, only another black look. The look was wasted, however, since by then Mr. Gould had turned away. He noticed us across the room, and came over. We had known him a long time; he was also one of our customers. Miss Laura had recommended us to him four years ago. When we told him why we were there, he smiled one of those dry little smiles that were almost his trademark.

"Yes, I'm sure her knitting will help her nerves. Poor thing, she'll feel worse when she hears about this. Tell her not to worry."

By the time we left Billings & Gould, we were two minds with but a single scheme. We knew where we wanted to go now. Once we'd dropped off the knitting, we would head straight for Mr. Gould's place, because that was where we would find Jessie Marshall. When his wife divorced him several years ago, Mr. Gould hired the cranky old woman to be his cook and housekeeper.

There were folks in Adamsport who would tell

you in all seriousness that Jessie Marshall was a witch.

One thing was sure, if Jessie *wasn't* a witch, she certainly had the looks for the part. She even backed Hester Thornton off the map in that department. Small and stooped, with little squinty eyes in a wrinkled face sour enough to make your lips pucker, she did a lot of ill-humored muttering. She even had the long pointed nose and chin that have always been associated with witches. Mr. Gould kept her on because she was a good housekeeper and cook and probably because he didn't have to pay her too much. He was not the free-spending type his partner was.

Jessie made pin money on the side. She was a home remedy specialist. She collected strange plants in the woods and combined them with stuff from her herb garden to use for various ailments people came to her to cure. They always had to cross her palm with a little silver — or paper would be more like it these days. This was what started the witch talk about her, but at the same time lots of those people swore by her remedies. I can testify to her success myself. One time when we were trimming some bushes, a hornet gave me a bad sting. Jessie mashed up a mess of some sort and put it on my sting. It took the pain out, and she didn't even charge me anything. I was surprised, because she didn't seem to like Wally and me, or anybody else except possibly her own family. Oh, yes, she had some family, a fact that really surprised us when we found out. She had a sister, and the sister had a daughter, and the daughter had two or three kids. We felt pretty sure that leftovers from Mr. Gould's larder often went to them without his necessarily knowing it.

But getting back to witchcraft: If you think it's all a thing of the past, and that nobody considers herself or himself a witch anymore, think again. Witchcraft has a long history in New England. When rumors started going around that some strange meetings were being held out at Thornton Farm, most Adamsporters laughed, but others shook their heads and said such goings-on shouldn't be allowed.

At the time the rumors began, we had discussed them at Wally's.

"Of *course* people have a sneaking belief in spooky things — the occult, the supernatural, all that stuff," J.G. had insisted. "For one thing, it's more fun than not believing. What's one of the most popular features in the newspaper? The daily horoscope column. You wouldn't believe some of the

27

people who read it every day. And how about those trashy tabloid newspapers you see in supermarkets? They run every sensational story about spooky doings they can get their hands on. People love it!"

Uncle Matt had been sitting in on that particular discussion. His jowls, his paunch, and his easygoing expression made him look like a country bumpkin, providing good cover for one of the sharpest law officers in the state.

"I expect you're right, J.G.," he had said mildly, "and if Adamsport wants to get a few thrills out of the idea that a coven of witches is coming together out at Thornton Farm, that's all right with me. I just don't want to see any witch hunts start. I know the ones who are showing up out there, and I'd classify them all as harmless kooks from our lunatic fringe — including the Thorntons."

His eyes twinkled in our direction.

"As for your Jessie, I'm not sure, because she can walk through the woods from Gould's place to Thornton Farm without being seen, but I think maybe she's giving them a try."

The fancy gateposts that marked off the entrance to Leonard Billings's estate were nearly half a mile on down Queen Anne's Road from Thornton Farm. Mr. Gould's place, an old restored New England farmhouse, was still farther on.

"I hope Jessie hasn't heard the news," said Wally. "If we can give her the blow-by-blow ourselves, maybe we'll get an idea of where she stands as far as the coven's concerned."

But when we turned into the drive there was no sign of Jessie anywhere, and no answer to Wally's knock when he banged on the back door. She didn't seem to be in her own quarters over the garage, either.

"Probably out in the woods digging up goodies," I said. And I was right. We got out the lawn mower and some garden tools and were hard at work when suddenly there was Jessie, standing watching us, with a basket on her arm and a trowel in her hand.

"You be careful not to nip off any blossoms in that flower bed like you did last time!"

Blossoms! I had happened to come too close to *one* flower when I was weeding last time, and of course Jessie had seen me do it. But then, her standard way of opening a conversation was to make some disagreeable remark, so we were used to it.

"I'll be careful," I said dutifully. Wally stopped the mower and we both walked over to her.

"Heard about the ruckus at Mr. Gould's office, Jessie?"

To our great satisfaction, she looked blank and said, "What ruckus?"

"Standish Thornton charged in and told Mr. Billings he isn't fit to live!"

We both watched carefully as her squinty old eyes slowly widened and narrowed again.

"Why'd he do that?" she mumbled, almost to herself. "Foolish!"

"It sure was. And we were there when it happened!"

Wally gave her the whole story, starting with the mix-up of the letters. She listened without comment, but her eyes flashed when she heard about the manhandling Thornton had undergone, and what she said then was interesting.

"They'll pay!" she muttered fiercely. "They'll pay!"

"Do you know Mr. Thornton, Jessie?"

"Of course! Ain't I been living on the same road as him and his sister for six years now?"

"Yes, but I mean — well, you know, all that squabble about Fletcher's Knoll —"

"*Squabble?*" Wally, and I don't think by accident, had picked the right word to set her off. "That's a sight more'n a *squabble!* Billings *stole* that property from the Thorntons, and he's going to pay for it, he's going to pay dearly before we're through! He —"

Witch or not, Jessie had made a slip, the sort we'd been hoping for.

We!

Wally started talking fast, as if he hadn't noticed.

"Well, I don't blame Mr. Thornton, because Mr. Billings is trying to cheat my dad the same way — the letter *he* was supposed to get was all about a claim Mr. Billings was making to some land Dad owns over in Compton — Dad says it's baloney and he isn't going to stand for it. . . ."

He babbled on, hoping she wouldn't notice we'd caught that "we." Watching her, I couldn't be sure.

"Well, anyway, I don't know what will happen to Mr. Thornton," Wally finished after a while, "but I don't see how they can do much to him, because he hadn't done anything more than scream at Mr. Billings before half the guys in the office jumped on him."

Naturally Wally didn't intend to add anything about how her employer had been the one who really brought Standish down, nor about what Standish had said to him. Just as well, too, because right then we heard a car turn into the driveway and stop, and a moment later Mr. Gould came walking around the side of the house. When he saw us, he didn't seem any too pleased. His lips thinned a little.

"Well, boys. I didn't expect to find you here. I suppose you've been giving Jessie all the news. Did you tell her about my part in it?"

"No, sir."

"Oh." His expression changed. He gave us an approving nod. "Good," he said, and turned to Jessie. "Jessie, I wanted you to hear it from me, before you got some secondhand report."

"Yessir," she mumbled, but glared at us for holding out on her.

"I helped to — er — get Mr. Thornton under control. It would have been worse for him if we hadn't stopped him before he did any real damage, but he didn't like it. He said, 'I won't forget this!' and I'm sure he won't, but perhaps when he's cooled off a bit he'll see that I only did what I had to."

Jessie's squinty old eyes slid away from him.

"Thornton's nothin' to me!" she claimed, which made Mr. Gould smile one of his dry little smiles.

"Perhaps not, but still, I wanted you to know."
He turned to us. "How did Miss Laura take the
news about the brawl?"

"About the way you'd expect, sir," I told him.
"She's sure that now she'll be forced to retire."

"Oh, I don't think it'll come to that," said Mr.
Gould. "Not quite yet. Well, I want to pick up
some papers in the house and then I'll be back at
the office."

He nodded to all of us and left us with Jessie
glaring at us again.

"You could've told me!"

"Jessie, it wasn't our place to talk about Mr.
Gould," said Wally, but as usual there was no
reasoning with her. She gave us a final glare, and
her parting words were, "Well, we ain't being
paid to gossip. Git on with your work! And mind
you don't butcher any more of my flowers!"

4

WE WENT TO WORK. ABOUT AN hour later I was guiding the mower around the far end of the lawn, and Wally was weeding and trimming a flower bed near the house, when I noticed him suddenly move over to a strip right under the kitchen windows. I knew the phone must have rung. After a minute or two he moved back to the first flower bed. He saw me watching, and made a series of signs. First, a finger to his lips. Next, an "okay!" sign with thumb and middle finger. Then one hand raised, palm toward me. He finished by making circles with one thumb.

I took this to mean, "Don't say anything. I got something! But don't stop, just go on working." So I kept my curiosity on a leash until he finally straightened up and motioned to me. I pointed the mower his way and stopped alongside him, leaving it in neutral to cover our conversation.

"Well?"

"I hoped it was someone calling her about Standish. Well, she mumbles so it was hard to get much, but I still hit pay dirt. I heard her say something about 'the Knoll — yes, yes, the Knoll!' as if she were impatient. I guess she's even bad-tempered with the other witches! Good thing, though, because that's where the pay dirt comes in. Right before she hung up, whoever was calling seemed to be repeating herself more than Jessie thought was necessary, because she said, 'Yes, yes, I *heard* you! Hour after new moon's down!' "

"Well! Wonder when it's new moon next?"

"We'll have to find out. Let's finish up here and eat lunch."

Minutes later we sat down in the shade and got to work on our sandwiches. Watching Wally eat is like watching a magician. Now you see it, now you don't. Worse yet, I knew it was a peanut butter and jelly sandwich. How anybody can swallow that mixture at all is beyond me, let alone swallow it whole. Especially when they could just as well have bluefish mixed with mayonnaise, like *my* sandwich. Of course, it happens that while Wally loves fishing he can't stand fish. I'm so-so about fishing, but I'll eat anything that crawls out of the sea. By the time he'd finished his third sandwich about a minute and a half later, he was giving me a nasty stare.

"How long is it going to take you to eat that stinking fish sandwich? It's polluting the air!"

"*Stinking?*"

"It's awful! I can hardly breathe!"

"Shut up and eat your cookies."

"I did."

"I must have blinked."

"Now, listen. If you ever finish chewing your cud, let's go check out that old trail to Fletcher's Knoll — remember the one we found way back when?"

I remembered.

"Must be seven or eight years ago now, but I'll bet it's still there."

Starting in those days, we had explored every path and trail we could find anywhere around Adamsport. Excitement tickled my spine. I stared at him hard.

"And why are you so hot to check out that old trail? Don't tell me. You're planning to attend a meeting."

Wally grinned, and nodded.

"From a distance. I'd like to get an idea of what

really goes on. Do they have plans for Leonard Billings? Some really nasty plans? And what will they do if their leader is in jail and can't make the meeting?"

A black night, with the moon gone down and witches on the Knoll . . . Who knew what their ideas of witchcraft might involve? Maybe, as Wally said, some really nasty plans that could lead to something serious. The shiver I felt now was more than a tickle. I knew that if we tried that trail to Fletcher's Knoll today, we'd be back for the coven's meeting.

We studied each other for a moment. Then I said, "Okay. Let's have a look."

The trail didn't run in from Queen Anne's Road, but from a side road, not much used and still just gravel, on the other side of the property. We stashed our bikes behind some bushes, then started looking. It took us a while even to spot the trail, and when we did the going was hard. Wally ducked branches and pushed aside bushes and grumbled, "It's grown up a lot since last time."

"Well, so have we."

It had never been much more than a deer trail, and looked as if even the deer had neglected it lately. But finally we came to the edge of a big stand of trees. There ahead of us was a rocky mound about forty feet high with a flat top and with hardly a blade of grass on it, let alone a shrub or tree. Fletcher's Knoll. We'd been two pretty scared nine-year-olds that first time. We'd heard the story about a man named Fletcher who had been found dead up on the knoll about a century and a half ago, savagely stabbed and slashed, with his blood running over the rocks like some animal's on a primitive altar. Later there had been reports of people seeing a ghost there. We hadn't seen any ghost, but we hadn't lingered long, either. We saw the knoll now with different eyes, but it was still grim and gloomy, with a sinister, blasted look about it.

Wally was in his element.

"If we sneak in carefully, without making a lot of noise, I don't see why we can't do it."

One more shiver explored my spine with icy tentacles.

"I'll give it some thought," I said.

We took care of another yard, old Mrs. Gunderson's, then split till after supper. The first thing I did at home was grab the *Old Farmer's Almanac*. My father kept a copy on a hook beside one of the bookshelves in his study — and heaven help any-

38

one who used it and didn't put it back. I hadn't made *that* mistake but once. Well, maybe twice. But not for a long time.

"Wow!"

A new moon was scheduled for Saturday night. Today was Friday.

"*Now* what are you up to?"

I cleared about a foot and a half straight up in the air. A father's voice can do that to you on certain occasions.

"A new record for the standing high jump," he observed. "What's got you so excited?"

I knew I was looking sheepish, so I took advantage of the fact. Wally's influence again.

"Well, I don't really believe in witches, but I can't help wonder what Standish Thornton and his gang might be up to come next full moon."

Full moon! A little fast footwork there.

"Is *that* it! Now, listen, if you and Wally are thinking of signing on for witchcraft prac-tice —"

I was glad he was taking it lightly.

"We won't! But did you hear about the battle at Billings and Gould, Dad? We were there!"

That got me off the hook. We went downstairs to supper and I told my parents the whole day's story — everything, that is, but a few minor details like Jessie's phone call and our visit to Fletcher's Knoll.

After supper I went to Wally's to talk about Saturday. He was outside, monkeying with his Yamakura. He was obviously pumped up, ready to go. I wondered how he was going to get through twenty-four hours of inaction before the big night. He looked at me and said, "Tomorrow night."

"Right."

"Moon sets at eight twenty-three."

"We must be reading the same almanac."

"By nine twenty-three it'll be pitch dark."

"Don't remind me. I'm skeered of the dark."

"Hear the six o'clock news?"

"Yes — but I hope Uncle Matt comes by."

"So do I."

The news report had left out more than it put in.

Uncle Matt did turn up. The only thing that took the edge off our pleasure was that he looked under the weather. His normally ruddy face was tinged with gray. Mrs. Brenner was instantly concerned.

"Matt, you've been working too hard! You don't look well. In fact, you haven't looked well all week!"

Like most people who are used to being healthy, he brushed this aside irritably.

"It's nothing, Edna. Had a touch of indigestion last night, but —"

"A *touch*? I talked to Nellie today, and she said it was a lot more than a *touch*. She almost called the Rescue Squad!"

"The woman is prone to exaggeration," growled Uncle Matt. "You know that."

"Well, she *did* call Dr. Briscoe."

"Yes, and he came, the pest!"

"And didn't he say —"

"He's on the trail of my gall bladder. It's his prime suspect. But I don't believe it."

"You'll be the *last* one to believe it, if I know you!"

"Now, don't pick on the man," said J.G. "He *is* my brother, no matter how depraved a life he's led."

"And put down that blueberry muffin, Matt!" said Mrs. Brenner. There was still a platter of blueberry muffins on the dining room table, and he could never resist her blueberry muffins.

"One won't hurt," he said, slathering a pat of butter on it. Before she finally called a halt by removing the platter, two more had disappeared.

Knowing we'd been on the scene, Uncle Matt

called for our version of what went on. We gave him every detail we could, including Slade's antics, which only made him grin.

"How about Standish, though, Matt?" asked J.G. "What *is* he up to? Do you really think he and Hester have decided they have special powers and stuff like that?"

"Probably. No question about it, Standish has gotten a lot more eccentric in the past year or so. But I don't think he's dangerous."

"He's a crack shot."

"Yes, I know, but I never heard of witches using firearms. He may be the star of the Target Club, but . . ."

The Target Club was an Adamsport institution. Its membership was made up of men and women devoted to pistol marksmanship. They had won competitions all over New England.

"I remember the time about a year ago when I met Ron Gould on the street looking more chipper than I'd seen him in a long time. He said, 'Matt, we won the Regional Cup last night in Boston, and Standish Thornton can take the credit. The man's a wizard with a target pistol!' Even then, Standish was pretty difficult, but they put up with him because of that."

"Well, I'll be interested to see if they still put up with him after this performance," said J.G. "Will Ron Gould feel he has to insist that Standish be thrown out of the club?"

I remembered the way Standish had looked at Mr. Gould, and said, "If I were Mr. Gould, I wouldn't want to be in the same place with Standish when he had a pistol in his hand, not after the way he said, 'I won't forget this!' "

After that, Uncle Matt brought us up to date on doings at the station, and at police court.

"Well, Slade brought him in, and then the judge had to decide what to charge him with. Which turned out to be a ticklish question," said Uncle Matt, obviously relishing that part of it. "After all, the only thing Standish did was open Leonard Billings's office door, not quite tearing it off the hinges, and shout at him. So it wasn't even simple assault, let alone something really serious like assault and battery. Disturbing the peace? Try and define that one. No, the only thing anyone could finally come up with was 'Trespassing,' and even that is pretty shaky in this case, where the man came into an office that anyone could enter during business hours. At any rate, we finally released him on his own recognizance, with a hearing set for Monday."

It is beyond me to describe the sensation this piece of news provided both of us. I don't know how we managed to sit still and not go straight through the ceiling. Standish Thornton was a free man, a free warlock, free to be present at and take charge of whatever went on Saturday night on Fletcher's Knoll. And Standish Thornton was fueled with a lot of new reasons to wage total war on Leonard Billings, using any weapons he might have in his shadowy but definitely dangerous arsenal.

Neither one of us could conceive of what might happen, but there was no question about one thing: Come what may, we would be taking our chances at the end of the path near Fletcher's Knoll tomorrow night.

In the meantime, Uncle Matt was saying, "Leonard Billings phoned and gave me a hard time, of course. First I got a lecture about how Standish was a maniac in our midst and I should take him seriously, but then when I asked if he'd like police protection at his home, that got under his skin — I knew it would — and he started blustering about how he could take care of himself. 'Well,' I said, 'if you can take care of yourself, then why are you calling me?' He hung up," said Uncle Matt, and we all had a good laugh.

That was the last good laugh we had for quite a while.

5

SATURDAY WAS ONE OF OUR REG-
ular workdays at Adamsport Village, as the waterfront restoration area was called. Old buildings
had been put back in shape — a ship chandlery,
a rope walk, and so on — and other old houses
had been moved to the site. Square-rigged ships,
schooners, and packet boats lay alongside the
wharves, along with all sorts of nineteenth-century
small craft. It was our biggest tourist attraction.

We put in five days a week there: Tuesday,
Wednesday, and Thursday working on the grounds,
Saturday and Sunday helping to handle the weekend crowds. That left us the other two days for
taking care of our own lawn-mowing accounts.

But this Saturday was not going to be just any
old Saturday. When I got to Wally's house, I

expected him to zoom out of his driveway as usual for the morning ride over to the Village. Instead, he came to the back door with a long face and beckoned me inside.

"Uncle Matt was rushed to the hospital in the middle of the night. They're going to operate as soon as possible."

You can imagine the state the family was in.

"Oh, to think it was my blueberry muffins that put him in the hospital! I'll never forgive myself!" moaned Mrs. Brenner. "I'll never forgive him, either!" she added angrily. "Pigging down one after another!"

"Three," said J.G.

"Three is one after another!"

"Edna, don't blame your muffins. It was only a matter of time before this would happen. And he's going to be all right. They take out gall bladders these days like there was nothing to it," said J.G., as much for his own morale as anyone's. "It's going to be all right. Doc Briscoe knows what he's doing, and he's finally got the old goat where he wants him! When this is taken care of, Matt'll be a new man!"

"Well, I hope so!"

We all hoped so. Wally and I took off for work in a decidedly subdued mood.

During the day he got word that Uncle Matt had been operated on and had come through all right. He would have to stay in the hospital for a couple of days and then take it easy for a while. At first we were so relieved and thankful that nothing else mattered. But then Wally found something to complain about.

"Now Slade will be the acting chief, and Uncle Matt won't be there to hold him down if he decides to start a witch hunt! We'll be lucky if he doesn't stage a raid on Fletcher's Knoll tonight and spoil everything."

"Whatever 'everything' turns out to be."

"Well, *something's* going to happen, and I'd like to see the show without him cutting it short!"

"Listen, Standish and the girls haven't exactly stuck handbills on telephone poles all over town announcing their meeting. They'll keep it to themselves if they can. I bet the word won't get to Slade. After all, not everybody works in the right flower bed — under the right window."

The new moon was low in the sky, a sliver of yellow against dark gray, when we took a run up Queen Anne's Road to see if we could spot any police cars lying low anywhere. All clear. As for the house at Thornton Farm, it couldn't be seen from the road, so we couldn't tell whether there was any activity there. We turned back and went around to the gravel road.

We walked our bikes the last quarter of a mile because we didn't want anyone to hear our motors stop near Fletcher's Knoll. By the time we stashed the bikes behind some bushes, the sky had clouded over and twilight had deepened into dusk, fuzzing the outlines of everything around us in that eerie way the last dying glimmers of daylight tend to do. Not a leaf stirred on a tree, not a twig moved on a bush. The stillness was oppressive and unnerving. It intensified every sound. Gravel crackled under our rolling tires like strings of firecrackers. We did our best to stay on the bare edges of the road, even though they shelved off into ditches and made the going tricky. We tiptoed more than walked, and spoke almost in whispers. It was the kind of quiet that always seems like a *listening* quiet, so that you get the paranoid feeling you're being overheard by someone or something hostile that considers you an intruder. Needless to say, this feeling is especially easy to come by when you *are* an intruder.

Trying harder than ever to move quietly, we ducked onto the path. It was more like a tunnel now than a path, because the thick tangle of branches above it and the bushes and undergrowth that surrounded it cut out almost all of the fading light that remained. For the first time it occurred to me to consider the return trip we would have to make in pitch darkness. Not a happy thought.

It seemed to take ten times as long to inch our way through as it had the first time. The night air was cool, almost cold, but we were both sweating by the time a patch of gray ahead told us we had reached the edge of the woods.

Fletcher's Knoll was no more than a vague, blurred mass in the gathering darkness. We checked our watches. By now the new moon had been down nearly half an hour. *Hour after new moon's down,* Jessie had said. We stretched out prone under the bushes beside the path and settled down to wait.

Waiting is not Wally's favorite activity. It's not high on my list, either, but for him it is torment. He sighed, he squirmed, he grumbled under his breath. He checked his watch ten times a minute. He complained about mosquitoes. Then, for something to do, he decided he was being eaten alive by ants. Army ants, to hear him tell it.

"Can't be ants. Ants don't stay up this late," I declared, though of course that's not true. Ants have no known bedtime.

Time seemed to be standing still, and nothing was happening. Had we misinterpreted Jessie's conversation? Was any meeting of the coven strictly a product of our imaginations? Or was there a meeting planned, or a ceremony, but not necessarily on Fletcher's Knoll? As one endless moment after another dragged past, we became more and more convinced we had picked the worst possible way to spend a Saturday night. The only thing that kept us there was the fact that neither of us wanted to be the one to suggest we give up and crawl away, defeated.

Over in the woods at the foot of the knoll, I saw a glimmer of light I thought was a firefly. I didn't even bother to say anything. But then I saw another firefly, and another.

"Look."

"I see 'em."

The fireflies came out of the trees into the open, bobbing along slightly, but now they looked more like candle flames, and dark figures were carrying them. A spasm of excitement, part triumph, part trembling, set a wild shiver through me from head to foot. I counted the candles as they kept coming, moving toward the base of the knoll, toward a corner that was out of our sight. Six, seven — eight candles. Not a full coven, which is twelve and a leader, but getting there.

Mounting the knoll from the far side, the figures began to appear on the long flat ledge that topped it, and now we could hear a droning sound, as if they were reciting something together, words we couldn't understand. They formed a circle on the knoll, and then a ninth dark figure, one carrying no candle, stepped into the center of the circle. Beside me I could hear Wally pull in his breath.

"It's him. It *is* him!"

Wearing the black robe we had seen before, the figure was unmistakable. He raised his arms, letting the long sleeves fall from them almost to the ground, and made a slow, complete turn in the center of his coven. The figures in the circle put their candlesticks on the ground and crouched beside them. Each was holding something small that gleamed in a waxy way, something they were rubbing with fingers they had spit on. I shivered as I realized the things were wax dolls, effigies of an enemy they were putting a curse on. Swaying and twisting, Standish Thornton made a tour of the circle, cupping his hands above each doll like a priest who'd gone mad, while his black robe slithered around him with the sinuous movements

52

of a snake. The sound of mumbling voices rose bit by bit, working toward a climax, as the circle parted and their leader walked with deliberate steps to the rim of the sloping ledge that faced in the direction of Leonard Billings's house.

Slowly, as though he were lifting a great weight, Standish Thornton raised his arms again until he looked like some enormous vampire bat ready to take off into the blackness of the night. He had raised them to their limit, and his coven's chorus had reached a hideous pitch, when all at once —

"Get off my property!"

A bullhorn. Leonard Billings with a bullhorn. From somewhere in the woods below, between the knoll and his house, Leonard Billings's deep, abrasive voice blasted the ceremony with a mocking and contemptuous order bawled through a bullhorn.

For an instant Standish Thornton froze, his arms still raised, as if he'd taken a bullet through his heart and his body had not had time to react. Then he seemed to plunge straight down the slope in front of him, and as he did every candle on the knoll was snuffed out. He and all the others vanished.

6

IN THE SUDDEN DARKNESS, THERE
was nothing. We could see nothing, not even the
knoll itself, nor each other. But we could still
hear Leonard Billings laughing, guffawing through
the bullhorn, rubbing it in. He finished his laugh,
and must have switched off the horn, because all
at once the stillness rolled back into place, rolled
over us and enveloped us and made us feel we
were suffocating.

In an atmosphere like that you either panic or
fight back with a feeble wisecrack.

"Show's over," I muttered. "Let's go, and beat
the crowd!"

We were both bracing ourselves for that blind
crawl through the black tunnel, the ordeal of feel-

ing our way, tripping over invisible roots and tangles, hoping we didn't stray off the path.

"I'm ready," said Wally somewhere in the darkness beside me. "Wanna go first?"

"Somebody better," I replied, but by then he'd gotten up his nerve to start. He never did take well to following. At the moment, I was just as glad.

"Come on," he said. "If you think I've missed a turn, let me know."

Would you believe neither of us had thought to bring a flashlight? Using one might have been risky, but at the same time, holding one hand over the lens, letting just enough reddish light seep around that hand to give us some idea of where we were, would have been quite a comfort. As it was, there was a good chance we might stray from the trail and start circling off through the underbrush in any direction. And somewhere in those woods was a powerful man in a black robe who was furious enough to do almost anything to anybody. And there was the coven. They had not looked like harmless old crones up there on the knoll. Where had they scattered to? If ever they got an inkling of the fact we'd been on the scene, we would have a lot of new enemies. That might have seemed laughable in broad daylight; it was a different matter when we were crawling on our bellies through thickets in the dark.

If we did get turned around, we might simply have to stop and wait till first daylight to get out of the woods. That part wouldn't have bothered us all that much in itself — but what about those parental watchdogs, Mr. and Mrs. J. G. Brenner and Mr. and Mrs. Charles W. Cunningham? If it got to be one or two o'clock and we hadn't showed up at home, they would not simply say, "Oh, well, they're probably having fun somewhere," and go back to bed. As I crawled on and on with these cheerful thoughts occupying my mind, I finally had to face the fact we'd made a wrong turn somewhere. No question about it. It was a gut feeling that went beyond any ordinary, rational deductions. I knew we were hopelessly lost.

That was the point at which Wally suddenly stood up ahead of me and said, "Well, here we are," and we stumbled out onto the gravel road. It only goes to show what I've always said: Never trust *anything* all the time, even gut feelings.

We didn't stop to talk things over. We walked our bikes down the road a way, thankful for the whiteness of the gravel, then hopped on and took off. We could have used something like a couple of chocolate frappes in a booth at Clem's, but the place would have been filled on a Saturday night with a lot of kids we knew, and we needed to talk privately. My folks were out to dinner, so we went to my house and fixed our own frappes.

"Well, how was that for an evening's entertainment?" I said as I got the ice cream out of the freezer.

"Worth the price of admission." Wally shook his head admiringly. "That Leonard Billings. He's a rat, isn't he? But you've got to give him credit — he's a master of timing."

"So was Standish and *his* supporting cast. The way they cut the stage lights — Broadway couldn't have done it better. Could you pick out Jessie, or Hester?"

"No. They all looked alike. But listen, did you see the way Thornton took off?"

"Could I miss it? He took off like a bat."

"Looked like one, too. But he *did* go down off that ledge like he was ready to stick pins in Billings personally! What do you suppose he did?"

I shrugged.

"Who knows? Unless he knew a path, he probably ended up in a bramble patch, picking stickers out of his tail."

It felt good to be back in familiar, normal sur-
roundings. We were so relieved we were full of
jokes and wisecracks. But at the same time, in
the back of our minds a dark area remained to
remind us that the things we had witnessed were
ugly, sinister, and possibly dangerous. I listened
to the comforting sound of the blender, gave the
frappes a good twenty seconds, decided they were
ready, and poured them out. Wally sipped his like
a connoisseur of fine wines, and made his judg-
ment.

"A good year, with a nice, round taste," he
decided. "So now what are we going to do?"

"You know as well as I do. As soon as he's
able to listen —"

"Right. We tell Uncle Matt about it."

"Right. Before we tell anyone else. He'll give
us a lecture, but he'll also be glad to have a
firsthand report, Wally. Because Billings will
tell Slade about this, and it'll be all over the
news."

"Only if Billings has a witness."

Wally had been doing some thinking, more
than I had at that point.

"What do you mean?"

"Listen, Les, he's a lawyer, so he's not going
to report a thing like this unless he has someone

to back him up. Otherwise Standish could deny everything and sue him. So if it comes out, that means he had someone with him. At least, that's the way I see it."

We kept checking the radio and TV newscasts all the rest of the evening, but nothing was reported about Fletcher's Knoll.

"So maybe he *didn't* have a witness with him," I said, after the midnight news.

But Wally had been doing more thinking. He shook his head.

"Hard to believe. He had a bullhorn with him. Why would he carry a bullhorn unless he had a pretty good idea something was going to happen up on the knoll, something he might want to blast with that horn? And if he knew all that — being a lawyer, wouldn't he take along someone to be a witness to whatever happened?"

I had to admit he had a point.

"For that matter, a guy like Billings would want an *audience*. But if that's the case, why hasn't he spread the story all over radio and TV?"

"Beats me, Les. He said in that letter to Standish that if they set foot on *his* property again he'd take 'appropriate steps.' Seems to me the first appropriate step he'd take would be to put all the heat he could on Standish and his witches. I just don't understand it."

But that's the way it was, and that's the way it stayed. The next morning, after not sleeping too well — strange dreams, what with Fletcher's Knoll and those frappes — I caught the seven o'clock news, and still heard nothing. My folks had come home late and weren't up yet. I had some breakfast and took off for work. As usual, I went by Wally's and we rode over to the Village together.

"Well, Wally, no news is still no news."

"I know. I listened, too."

"When can we see Uncle Matt?"

"Not till after work. J.G. and Mom are going over around eleven, but Doc Briscoe doesn't want him to have more than two visitors at a time, and not many of those."

On our lunch hour Wally phoned home to get a report. J.G. said Uncle Matt looked pretty fair, everything considered.

"Grumpy as a bear, which Doc Briscoe takes as a good sign. But of course, it's no joke, going through a thing like that. He'll have to take it easy for a while."

We finished work at four-thirty, and went straight to the hospital.

Uncle Matt's impersonation of a grumpy bear was right on target, but he dropped it long enough to seem glad to see us. We offered the usual hearty comments — "Hey, you look fine!" "Yeah, great!" — but he wasn't having any of it.

"I do not. I look like I've been dragged through a knothole. What have you two squirts been up to?" Already, in one minute's time, his practiced eye had spotted something guilty in our expressions. As I said before, behind his country-cop exterior was a lot of first-class police savvy. Wally and I looked at each other. We had to grin.

"What a suspicious guy he is!" I said.

"Terrible!" agreed Wally. "Well, Uncle Matt, it just happens that —"

"Yes, I know how things 'just happen' to you two! What is it now?"

For openers, Wally gave him a rundown on Jessie and the phone call. The instant he finished that part, his uncle was ready with a deduction.

"Don't tell me. I can guess! Last night, after the moon was down, two nosy kids were hiding in the bushes. I remember the time, when you were little twits, you came home bragging about

61

sneaking in through the woods from Verney Road —"

"Is that the name of that gravel road, Uncle Matt? I never noticed, did you, Les?"

Bear-growl from Uncle Matt. He rolled his eyes up like a martyr.

"Give me strength!"

Wally went poker-faced.

"Well, if you'd rather not hear what we saw there, Uncle Matt, we sure wouldn't want to upset you by telling you —"

"Don't you pull any of your father's stuff on me, you pipsqueak! Just get on with it!"

Between us we put together a detailed account of exactly what went on at Fletcher's Knoll. Uncle Matt was always a good audience, because when you were telling him something like that he listened intently, reserving his comments for later. His only interruptions were a few terse, pertinent questions.

By the time we finished, he had actually mellowed a bit. He lay back against his pillows and let us off easy.

"Well, I've got to admit, I can't blame you too much for wanting to be there. In your place, I guess I'd have been there, too. I'm glad to have the straight story up my sleeve, in case anything comes of this."

"What do you suppose Thornton did when he went charging down off the knoll, Uncle Matt?"

"Probably fell on his face." Uncle Matt was enjoying himself now, his eyes glinting as he thought of angles. "What I'd like to know is, how did Billings find out that something was set for Fletcher's Knoll last night?"

"And why didn't he tip off the police and have them there ready to arrest everybody?" said Wally, but that only made his uncle shake with laughter.

"Are you kidding? Can you see that gang of mine trying to arrest nine witches in the pitch dark? Why, they'd end up looking like a bunch of Keystone Kops in an old two-reel comedy! That sort of caper can backfire badly, and Billings would know that. No, I have a couple of other ideas. For example, Billings *could* have had Slade and a man or two along, ready to grab Thornton if he tried to attack him, but somehow I doubt that. On the other hand, suppose he hotfooted it back to his house, barricaded himself in, and called the police, hoping Thornton would come up and try to get at him again. He'd love to see Thornton in the slammer, out of his hair, no doubt about that. . . . Of course, if Leonard Billings makes any charges against Thornton and his gang, and Thornton tries to deny anything went on, *you* might have to give evidence."

"What? You mean — tell all this to *Slade?*"

"Yes."

This was a jolt. Even though we *were* snoopers, we didn't like the idea of being portrayed as such in the news reports. Uncle Matt's eyes glinted again as he enjoyed our squirming.

"As you'll find in the lawbooks, a witness has a duty to give evidence. He can be compelled to do so by a subpoena that orders him to the witness stand, and if he doesn't he can be put in jail. So the next time you're inclined to stick your noses into something, remember what you're letting yourself in for."

Then he let up a little.

"But don't worry. It wouldn't be as bad as you think. Most people wouldn't blame you — they'd like to have been there themselves."

"Standish and his gang would blame us plenty!" I pointed out. "I'd be nervous every time we rode past the farm. And I hate to think how Jessie would act!"

"Well, I don't see why Billings would need us, anyway," said Wally, and gave Uncle Matt his theory about why the lawyer would have had a witness along. When he had finished, his uncle nodded thoughtfully.

"Not bad. Not bad at all. Unless he walked down to the knoll on the spur of the moment — it's only five minutes or so from his house — he probably *would* have taken someone along. On the other hand, let's say he got a last-minute tip-off on the phone from someone. And for that matter, would he be home alone on a Saturday evening? He's the kind who's usually out partying somewhere."

"And besides that, why hasn't he made a complaint yet? What's he waiting for?"

By now, of course, we were all three of us simply enjoying ourselves, trying out ideas about a local squabble that was pretty trivial, and more comical than otherwise. That moment sticks in my mind in every detail. I can remember the big pot of yellow chrysanthemums someone had sent, and the books and magazines Aunt Nellie had brought over, and Uncle Matt's steel-rimmed spectacles balanced on top of them, and the way he looked, tipped up in his hospital bed, his round, jowly face haggard against the white pillows but looking better now that he was having fun, and I can remember the way he squinted at his watch and then reached for the switch on his bedside radio as he said, "Well, let's check the five o'clock news and see if anything's leaked out yet. . . ."

He hit it right on the button. The announcer's voice was taut with excitement.

"The body of a prominent Adamsport attorney, Leonard Billings, has been found near his home on Queen Anne's Road. He had been shot twice, once in the head and once through the heart. We will interrupt with further details as soon as they are available."

7

WE MUST HAVE LOOKED LIKE
figures in a wax museum. Uncle Matt with his
arm outstretched, his finger still on the switch,
the two of us bolt upright on the edges of our
chairs, none of us moving a muscle.

Then Uncle Matt sagged back against his pillows and let out his breath in one big gust.

"Good God!"

He snapped off the radio and his face set unhappily.

"Billings *murdered!* Terrible! . . . And what a
time to be stuck here! Slade and that hotshot pros-
ecutor of ours will make a three-ring circus out
of this!"

We knew whom he meant. The assistant attorney general Carl Fry was a headline-hunter

with political ambitions. Here was a murder case that was sure to get national attention. A coven of witches? A sinister ceremony in the black of night? It couldn't miss! If Fry and Slade bagged the murderer it could be the making of both their careers. Uncle Matt looked our way and added the words we had been dreading.

"Well, that does it. You've got to tell Slade what you know right away." He glared at the phone beside the radio. "They cut off my phone. Said I mustn't have calls, or make them. So you'll have to go out and phone from the desk. If Slade's at the station, tell him I'm sending you down with information. And when you get there, tell him to give you a rundown on what's gone on, to bring back to me. I don't expect him to come over here when a case like this is breaking, but I want to be kept up to date!"

We left him turning on the radio again, frowning and brooding and growling about being stuck in the blankety-blank hospital. We got right through to Slade, who told us to hurry over. Needless to say, we were kicking ourselves all the way to our bikes, wishing we'd never gone near Fletcher's Knoll in the first place. We could foresee reporters and TV jerks interviewing us, and the prospect had us squirming like two worms. Being partners to a witch-hunt was not something we were going to be proud of, and we knew that was what Slade and Fry would make out of all this. They would nail Standish Thornton for the murder if they possibly could, to the applause of millions. There have always been plenty of folks who glory in a good witch hunt.

Adamsport's police station, on Willow Street, was erected over a hundred years ago by a generation that liked public buildings to look official. It was built like a fortress out of heavy blocks of gray granite, and the entrance was flanked by a pair of round frosted lamps on six-foot-high standards, with POLICE painted on them in black letters. We had been there often, we'd wangled tours of the whole building, including the jail cells, and we'd always known every man on the force. When we walked in, the man on the desk was Eddie Soares, Uncle Matt's favorite cop. Eddie was Portuguese, with bright black eyes in a smooth face that never seemed to grow a day older. He welcomed us with his usual warm grin.

"Hey, the lieutenant's waiting for you guys."

"We came as fast as we could without being picked up for speeding."

"Yeah, I've seen you on those wheels of yours. How's the chief?"

"Looking good, considering."

By that time Slade had poked his head through the door to the back rooms.

"Thought I heard you." He jerked his head at us, a man in a hurry. "Come tell me what you've got."

We followed him to Uncle Matt's office, where he'd obviously installed himself. He had the good grace to look a little sheepish and offer a half apology.

"More room in here, and I'm going to need it while *this* is going on. Carl, meet Wally Brenner and Les Cunningham. They've been around this station longer than I have!"

Prosecuting Attorney Carl Fry was sitting in an armchair in front of Uncle Matt's desk, with his big square teeth set like a vise, holding a cigar a foot long. Now, Slade wasn't a bad guy, just young and cocky, but Fry was something else. He was a tall, handsome, blond type built like a fullback (which he had been, All-Star), with pale blue eyes that were ruthlessly fixed on the main chance, the sort of man who saw himself as headed for the governor's mansion, and after that the White House. Looking at him, I wouldn't have wanted to be Standish Thorton. Fry stuck out his hand and gave us both a candidate's handshake and a big smile.

"Glad to see you, boys. If Chief Brenner says you have something for us, I know it must be important," he said in a patronizing way that set my teeth on edge. Obviously he wasn't really expecting much.

Wally turned to Slade and gave him Uncle Matt's message, word for word. Slade nodded earnestly.

"Sure, sure — tell him I'd have sent word of this to the hospital sooner, only we decided they might not want him to be bothered. I'll give you everything we know so far, and you can bring him up to date."

Fry sent Slade a sideways look, and muttered dubiously.

"You sure that's wise? I mean, I'm sure these boys are dependable and all that, but —"

"Listen, Carl, you don't have to worry about them, they know enough not to talk out of turn — you can depend on his uncle for that!" said Slade, pointing to Wally. As I said, Slade wasn't a bad guy. "Besides, I haven't even got a man free to send over to the hospital, let alone run over there myself."

Fry shrugged and nodded.

"Okay. He's the chief. Gotta keep him posted," he added, and I didn't care for the snide way he said *that*, either. "Well, anyway, what is it you have to tell us, boys?"

I looked at him and thought, okay, you asked for it, we'll give it to you!

And we did. When we told them what we'd seen, they almost fell out of their chairs. They all but jumped up and did a war dance. In fact, Fry *did* jump up, and began rubbing his hands together like a happy executioner.

"Wow! This is terrific! Terrific! This practically wraps it up! Everything fits now!"

"Even the bullhorn! We wondered about that. Well, I've got to get going again, so we'll have to make this quick," said Slade.

"Let me give them the meat of it, Al." Fry leaned forward importantly in his chair. "Now, there's probably a slug in Billings's head, but the one that went through his heart was in the ground right under the body. And whaddaya know? — it was a 'twenty-two long rifle slug, the kind they use in their target pistols! Well, you probably know that Thornton's the star of the Target Club —"

"Yes."

"— and another club member is Sergeant

McClure of this here now police department, and McClure is a ballistics nut. He's done a lot of work matching up slugs with the guns they came from — you know, every gun barrel's rifling leaves its own marks on a slug. Almost like fingerprints. Well, a few years ago, just because it was a chance to play with his hobby, McClure did a study of Target Club slugs and kept a record of them. Thornton probably forgot all about that, if he even knew. So after we found this slug under the body, McClure remembered those old records of his. He got them out — and whaddaya know? — the slug matched the records for Thornton's target pistol! He handed us his report just before you got here."

Slade stood up.

"And now I'm going out to the farm and tell Thornton we're rounding up every 'twenty-two we can locate, and ask him for his pistol. And if he doesn't look around and discover he can't seem to find it anywhere, I'll be surprised! So why don't you boys hop back to the hospital with your report, and tell the chief I'll let him know how I make out with Thornton. By the way, one more thing. Did you hear anything that sounded like shots?"

When we both said we hadn't, he shrugged.

"Well, you may have been clear out on the road and gone by then. A gun like that wouldn't make a lot of noise, and if anyone did hear it from a distance they'd probably think what most people think when they hear a gun go off — car backfiring somewhere."

Fry gave us a calculating look.

"Have you told anyone else about last night?"

"Only Uncle Matt."

"I told you they keep their mouths shut," said Slade.

"Well, that's good. Then, for the moment, we'll all keep your evidence under our hats, okay? Give Thornton a chance to hang himself still further by denying that any shenanigans took place on Fletcher's Knoll last night."

"Fine with us!" Wally could not help saying, and certainly this *was* good news. At least we wouldn't be dragged into the open quite yet.

We left the station in a state of shock. Things were moving so fast we felt numb.

"Well, it looks like Thornton is *it*."

"It sure does. If they find his gun out there, they've got him, and if he claims it's disappeared, they've got him anyway."

"For those two, it's the dream murder case. Brilliant police work! An open-and-shut case for the prosecution."

At the hospital we found a dragon on the desk in the hall, a tough old head nurse who didn't take any nonsense from anybody. The name-plate on her starched uniform read, "Freda Wagner, R.N."

"Your uncle's had his supper and now he's asleep. If he's awake at seven o'clock, maybe you can see him, but not before."

Only by a great effort of will did Wally contain himself. He gave the dragon a deeply respectful look and said, "Gee, I'm glad he's resting. Lieutenant Slade sent us over with some important news for him about the Billings murder, but it can wait."

A pair of dragon's ears had perked up.

"News?" she said, and her rimless glasses bobbed a little on her nose as she talked. "You mean, there are new developments?"

Just from the way she spoke you could tell she read all those sensational tabloids for sale in the supermarkets. Wally looked this way and that down empty corridors, and lowered his voice.

"There sure are. We can't say anything till we've seen Uncle Matt, but . . ."

"Oh, my! Well . . . maybe in a few minutes we might be able to . . . Let's wait for just a little while and then I'll check on him."

"Great!" We could see Uncle Matt getting a sharp nudge from Nurse Wagner within a very short time. "We'll wait right here," said Wally, and we sat down in the small waiting room near the desk.

The head nurse may have been dying of curiosity, but we were wrong about the sharp nudge. She was also incurably conscientious. She checked Uncle Matt three times and came back each time with a long face.

"Still asleep."

We waited a long, long time, but then something happened I'm sure Nurse Wagner would never forget. Neither would we. Everything started when she answered the desk phone.

"Nurse Wagner. *What?*" Oh! Oh, my goodness! Yes . . ." (swift glance at a chart), "yes, I've got four-o-two. I'll have it ready!"

She sent a nurse's aide running, then with her eyes popping told us, "They've just brought in Standish Thornton in a violent state, they had to give him a tranquilizer, and now they're bringing him up here!"

With that she took off down the corridor. We heard the elevator come up, and watched a light ping on above the elevator doors. One set of doors opened, and out poured a cop named Weedon, two orderlies and a young intern, with Thornton Standish strapped onto one of those stretchers on wheels. He was twitching feebly, but that was all. The group went past us down the corridor. We stared at each other, flabbergasted. Uncle Matt's room was 404, and even-numbered rooms were on the same side of the corridor.

"Wally!" I said. "Don't tell me Thornton Standish is going to end up in the *next room* to Uncle Matt!"

8

WE LOOKED DOWN THE COR-
ridor, wishing we had nerve enough to follow the
procession. They all trooped into Room 402, except for Officer Weedon, who stayed in the door-
way. After a while Nurse Wagner came out, still
flushed and excited, and shut the door after her.
Weedon took up his post alongside it. She saw
us, backtracked a few steps for a look into Uncle
Matt's room, gave us the high sign, and disappeared into his room. We weren't far behind.

"He's waking up," she said. "All that commotion! — enough to wake anyone!"

Uncle Matt was stirring, blinking, snuffling,
like someone coming up out of a deep, deep sleep.
I wondered if they hadn't slipped him a sleeping
pill somewhere along the line.

"Wha's tha'? Wha's goin' on?" he asked in a thick voice, and tried to sit up.

"Now, just a minute, Matt!"

Nurse Wagner scolded him, cranked up the head of his bed, and plumped up his pillows. His eyes focused somewhat vaguely on us, and he said, "You still here?"

"No, we just came back."

He shook his head, yawned, and came around a little more.

"Back?" He scowled, concentrated with a mighty effort, and the fog seemed to clear away a bit. His eyes sharpened. "Oh, yes. Been to the station. Been to see Slade. Did you tell him —?"

Wally nodded. Suddenly Uncle Matt was more alert. He glanced at Nurse Wagner and then at us.

"Don't you worry about Freda Wagner," he told us. "She knows more about what goes on in this town than anybody, and she keeps her mouth shut."

She gave him an affectionate glare.

"I'd love to stay, but I'm busy. You've got a new neighbor, Matt. Standish Thornton's in the next room."

That *really* woke him up.

"*What?*"

"Boys'll tell you," she said, and bustled out,

closing the door behind her. Uncle Matt grinned, and it was good to see him do it.

"She's the best," he said. "Well, now, what's this all about? What's going on here?"

We reported on our talk with Slade and Fry, and told him about Standish Thornton showing up on a stretcher. He was about to comment when there was a tap at the door.

"See who that is, Les."

It was Lieutenant Slade, looking like someone who had won a million-dollar jackpot in the state lottery. He came in and planted himself at the foot of the bed.

"Matt, you're looking great!" he began, which got him a sardonic snort from the patient. "Did the boys tell you ——?"

"They brought me up to date. *Now* what's happened? What's Thornton doing here?"

Slade held up his hand.

"Let me start at the beginning. I took a couple of men and drove to Thornton Farm. Hester Thornton came to the door, with her brother right behind her. They came outside. And I noticed right away that Thornton had a lot of scratches on his hands and face.

"I asked if they'd been home last night. She spoke up before he could say anything. She said,

'Yes. We were together all evening.' From what the boys said, I knew that was a lie. I don't think she followed him down that slope!

"I asked them if they'd heard any commotion during the evening, over in the direction of Fletcher's Knoll. They looked at each other, and he said, 'What are you getting at?'

"I said, 'Just answer the question, please, and I'll tell you.'

"Well, about then he seemed to decide we might know something about the doings on the Knoll, because he tried to cover himself. He said, 'We did meet briefly with some friends, but there was certainly no "commotion." '

"I said, 'And you didn't hear any noises anywhere else? Any shots?'

"That seemed to bother him. He even stammered when he said, 'Shots? Certainly not!'

"Then I asked him, 'Have you heard about Leonard Billings?'

"He hesitated just a little before he said, 'Billings? What about him?'

"I said, 'His body's been found not far from Fletcher's Knoll.'

"Thornton never changed expression. He said, 'What's that to me?'

"I said, 'Well, he was shot with a 'twenty-two-caliber weapon. We're picking up every 'twenty-two pistol or rifle we know anything about, so we'd like to have your target pistol, please.'

"When I said that, he came on strong. I mean, the man was practically foaming at the mouth. '*My* target pistol? Are you suggesting *I* might have *shot* that swine? How dare you?' He really laid into me, called me everything he could think of, and I was about to stop being polite when he shouted, 'All right! Take it and be damned!' He pushed past us and marched over to an old heap parked in the drive. He jerked open the door on the passenger side, jerked open the glove compartment, and — What did I say, boys? Didn't I say he'd pull that one? Sure enough, he turned around and yelled, 'It's gone!'; and with that he went absolutely bananas. He tried to say more, but he was so mad he was choking. He raised his fists in the air and came straight at me. Me! Why me? Anyway, we grabbed him, and it took all three of us to wrestle him down — he's a powerhouse, that one. For that matter, we had to hold her off, too, that sister of his, and for an old lady, *she* was no slouch.

"By the time we got the cuffs on him we knew this was where we'd have to bring him, not the station house. So we did, and when we got to the emergency room they gave him a shot — it was like giving a wild animal a shot, only that would have been easier, if they could have popped a dart into him from a distance! But anyway, that knocked him out, and now he's next door, strapped in, and I'm going to leave a man outside the door around the clock — right, Matt? For one thing, I want to be sure he doesn't get any funny ideas about *you*, if he finds out you're here!"

Uncle Matt nodded.

"Sounds like Thornton's pretty far around the bend." His eyes probed Slade's with the sort of look we were used to seeing. "But do you really think he could have shot Billings? If he'd been strangled, or battered to death, or even shot six times, I wouldn't doubt it was Thornton for a minute. But would a madman — assuming he's that — would a madman put just two bullets in him, in just the right places?"

Slade gripped the rail at the end of the bed, hands wide apart, the way a preacher grips his lectern when he leans forward to make a point from the pulpit.

"Matt, you know as well as I do, nobody can be more cold-blooded and calculating and careful about the way they kill someone than a nut. The man is crazy enough to do anything! He may never stand trial, but at least we got him off the streets!"

Streets didn't seem to have much to do with Thornton Farm or Fletcher's Knoll, but never mind. As far as Lieutenant Slade was concerned, he'd wrapped up a great piece of police work. Uncle Matt, hardly in shape for a full-scale debate, looked weary and defeated. He raised one hand, and let it fall.

"Okay, Al. You've done a great job. Thanks for coming by."

"Oh, that's okay, Matt — I wanted to check next door anyway and make sure everything was under control," said Slade. Tact was not his strong point. He glanced at his watch. "Well, gotta get going — those newshounds are already on our trails, waiting downstairs for a statement. I'll keep you posted, Chief!"

He included the three of us in an all-purpose wave and was gone, eager to stand in front of those microphones and give a waiting world the news. He left a heavy silence behind him.

For a long time Uncle Matt glowered into space, not saying a word. And because we knew enough to keep our mouths shut at a time like that, we didn't say anything, either. Finally he squirmed around, winced at a twinge of pain, and put his thoughts into words.

"A murder done by a witch! Makes a great story, national publicity, so Al and Fry can't see anything else. They don't *want* to see anything else! And maybe it's all true. But still, they ought to check out every possible angle, by way of doing a thorough job. If Al was completely on his own, he just *might* stop and think about it. But with Fry urging him on, there's not a chance. It's a shame. . . ."

He was looking very tired again, his eyes heavy, his body slumping down.

"I wish I could . . . Well, I can't, and that's that."

"Take it easy, Uncle Matt, and don't worry about it," said Wally, suddenly concerned. "The important thing right now is for you to get some rest."

I said, "Sure! In a couple of days you'll be out of here, and on your way to —"

"On my way to retirement, if those boys have anything to say about it," snapped Uncle Matt with a brief show of the old feisty spirit.

"Not a chance! Well, we'll bring J.G. up to date, so he won't pester you with too many questions when they come by later on."

Uncle Matt nodded and closed his eyes, and we tiptoed out, easing the door shut behind us.

"How is he?" Weedon wanted to know. Wally said, "Okay. Tired, but okay."

When we reached the desk, Nurse Wagner gave us a sharp look.

"I was about to come after you. He's had enough visitors for a while."

"That's for sure," I said. "He was dropping off before we even got out of the room."

"He's been through more than he's willing to admit."

"Before my folks come over," said Wally, "I'll have them call you to see if it's okay."

"Do that."

"How's Mr. Thornton?"

"No problem."

As we were walking out to our bikes, Wally's jaw was set hard. I think it was all he could do to keep from crying. When he spoke, he bent forward a little as if his stomach was in a knot.

"It just *kills* me to see him like that! Having to lie there, knowing what ought to be done, and not being able to lift a finger to do it!"

"I feel the same way," I admitted. "He'd at least check up on where a lot of other people were last night. He'd even check up on Mrs. Billings, to make sure she's really in Maine."

"And he'd want to know where Mr. Gould spent his evening. After all, he lives close by."

"And Cynthia, the office sexpot — he'd want to know where she was, too."

That made Wally grin a little.

"Can you see her out in the woods in her high heels, ruining her makeup?"

"No, I can't — but Uncle Matt would make sure, just the same. It's hard to see how it could be anybody but Standish, but he wouldn't take it for granted, the way Slade and Fry are doing."

"It's a pain. A real pain. If only we —"

"Now, hold it, Wally! There's nothing we can do *this* time. *We* can't run around checking alibis. All we'd get out of that would be big trouble from Uncle Matt."

"I know. But I'd still give anything if . . . Well, come on, let's go home."

At Wally's I called home and spent some time explaining why I hadn't showed up for supper, while Wally did the same for his folks. They admitted we had a pretty fair excuse.

Mrs. Brenner put dinner on the table for us, and they sat with us while we ate.

"Poor Matt," she said. "I wish he wouldn't fret over this business. I know he'd be checking everything, as usual, if he could — but how can it be anyone *but* Standish Thornton? He must have gone off his head."

"And shot Billings just twice, neat and tidy?" said Wally. "Slade talked about how cold-blooded madman murderers can be, but Uncle Matt wasn't satisfied. He always says the first thing to look for in a murder is: Who benefits? I can't see Standish really gaining anything, even if he got away with it. Shooting Billings wouldn't get back Fletcher's Knoll. So unless he just killed him in a rage . . ."

"Which, for want of a better explanation, is what it looks like," said J.G. "It's a shame, though, because I know Matt will never feel right about this."

There was a glum silence for a moment. Then Wally asked, "Has there been anything more on the news yet?"

"Not much. Lots of sideshows going on, of course. The grieving widow has been notified, and Ron Gould is going to fly to Maine to bring her back."

"He'll like that. He's always had a yen for her, from what I hear," said Mrs. Brenner.

"You women are such gossips," said J.G.

"What are you talking about? Come to think of it, I heard it from *you!*" she said, giving us all a laugh. Out in the kitchen the teakettle even joined in with a whistle. "I'm making more coffee," she added. "Wally, would you go pour some water through the filter?"

Wally jumped up and went to the stove. But then, while he stood there, the kettle kept on whistling. His mother glanced around at him.

"Wally, what are you doing?"

When she spoke he jumped.

"Huh? Nothing. I was just thinking," he muttered, and poured the water. While we were still eating, J.G. phoned the hospital. Nurse Wagner told him they could come over for a few minutes. I waited till we heard them drive away before I asked the obvious question.

"Okay — what was that business with the teakettle?"

I had already noticed that since he had returned to the table he'd been picking at his food, which was certainly not his normal style. He looked like someone who'd had a bad shock, and was struggling to deal with it.

"Well, it was the darnedest thing. . . . With all the other stuff that's been going on, you wouldn't think I'd still have that letter mix-up on my mind . . ."

"The what? Oh — that!" That silly business with the letters seemed like something that had happened long ago. "So?"

"Well, off and on I've wondered if somehow someone in the office *could* have opened those envelopes and switched the letters around, after all. So I was looking at that teakettle, with all the steam coming out of it, and I remembered something Laura said when she was telling us what she did that morning at the office. You remember, she took coffee to Billings, and then filled Mr. Gould's electric pot with water and took it to him, because he liked to heat the water and make his tea himself. . . ."

9

I FELT AS IF I'D BEEN PLUGGED INTO a live outlet myself.

"Mr. Gould? Are you saying Mr. Gould could have switched those letters?"

"It's possible. Lots of people have steamed open letters, and then resealed them, and nobody the wiser. Suppose he was looking for a chance to make Thornton even madder at Billings than he already was —"

"The letter he was supposed to get would have done that."

"But something extra, like switching the letters, so that someone else would read his first and could talk about it, would make him twice as mad!"

"You mean, mad enough to kill Billings, if

that's what Mr. Gould wanted? Are *you* crazy? Can you see him doing something as — as *silly* as that?"

Wally always hated to give up on an idea, but he had to face the fact that this one was a dud. He threw up a hand as if he were brushing away a gnat.

"Oh, forget it. You're right. It wouldn't be Mr. Gould's style. But that's only part of it. When that teakettle started me thinking, a lot of things hit me all at once. Mom says she's heard Mr. Gould has always had a yen for Mrs. Billings. Laura says Mrs. Billings doesn't believe in divorce, and Billings didn't want one, either. So if those two things are true, then the only solution for Mr. Gould was to have something happen to Billings."

The whistling teakettle had come up with a ridiculous possibility neither of us could believe in, but in the process it had turned loose a suspicion that *didn't* seem ridiculous, and wouldn't go away now. Suddenly we were staring at each other and I was saying, "And maybe when Standish *did* come charging in looking like he wanted to kill Billings, maybe *that's* when Mr. Gould began to get ideas!"

For a moment Wally didn't say anything. He

looked as if he wished he'd *never* said anything. We were talking about a man we'd always respected, a man who had been fair to us, a man who paid us money to work for him, the last man either of us would ever have associated with any kind of lawbreaking, let alone murder. And yet . . .

"He has a motive, all right," said Wally. " 'Who benefits?' . . ."

"And there's that other thing they always say in detective stories, that French saying. *Cherchez la femme.*" I said, putting two years of high-school French behind my effort to say it correctly.

"That's right. 'Look for the woman.' "

Anyone who had read a dozen crime novels knew that one.

Now other bits and pieces began to fall into place, thick and fast, and we began to mention them in somber tones, not liking what we were saying, but knowing we couldn't pretend the thoughts were not there.

"Mr. Gould is big in the Target Club, Wally. I think Uncle Matt said something once about him being the club's secretary, didn't he? So he must have known about the ballistics study. And if he did, he would know McClure would think of it right away when they found that 'twenty-two slug under the body. Suppose, somehow, he got hold of Standish's pistol . . ."

"Sure. And one of the things bothering Uncle Matt is that business of those two neat shots, especially that second one through the heart. When you think of it, that was one way of making *sure* the slug would be found, either in the body or the ground."

"And remember your idea that Billings would have had someone along, to be a witness? If there *was* someone, we know now it wasn't Slade or any other policeman, so why not Mr. Gould?"

"And another thing — why *was* Billings home at that time on a Saturday night? He must have known ahead of time about Fletcher's Knoll. Who told him? Mr. Gould could have known about it, because of Jessie."

Ideas were coming at us from all directions. Here was the sort of thing Uncle Matt had talked about: an angle that ought to be checked out. But . . .

"Mr. Gould! Gee, I don't know. I hate to think about it," I admitted. But then a new thought made me feel better. "Well, anyway, we shouldn't have to wonder long. All we've got to do is find out he spent the evening with friends, and we're home free. We can forget all about this."

Wally gave me a queer look.

"You're right. But tell me something, just for instance. Can you see him doing a thing like this?"

I closed my eyes and thought about him. I thought about how different he was from Billings, how outwardly mild and colorless, and how abrasive Billings must have been at times, how much Mr. Gould might have grown to resent and dislike him, even hate him, especially when a woman he had a thing about was trapped with the man. I also remembered how unflappable he was, how cool he'd been during the fracas with Standish, how fast he'd moved when he had to. And I remembered another thing Uncle Matt had often said: Some of the most proper people you'd ever meet anywhere were murderers.

I opened my eyes and, even though the words tasted bad in my mouth, I said, "Yes, I can."

Wally nodded unhappily.

"So can I. He's just cool enough to plan the whole thing, step by step — and if we're right, he got every break in the book and is probably home free."

By now we were both feeling terrible. But what could we do? We couldn't just walk away from the whole business, simply because we thought more of Mr. Gould than we did of Standish. Wally put it into words.

"Well, Mr. Gould has always seemed okay to me, and I can't say as much for Standish — but if Standish *didn't* kill Billings, he shouldn't take the rap for it. He's entitled to a fair shake the same as everybody else. And right now, in spite of a creep like Fry, he's innocent until proven guilty. So . . . what are we going to do about it?"

I had to laugh at that question, but not because it was funny. I simply stared at Wally and sort of laughed.

"You know darn well what we're going to do. If Uncle Matt were running the show right now, it would be different, because he'd be doing just what he was talking about — he'd be checking everything. But he's not in charge, and he hasn't got anybody in his corner but us. So we're going to do as much as we can without making anyone suspicious, or getting into trouble, and if it looks like we're off on the wrong track, then that's that."

"And Lord help us if we blow our cover and Uncle Matt gets wind of this!"

I agreed, but I could think of a possibility even worse than that. What if Mr. Gould somehow caught onto the fact that we were trying to check him out? I thought about his controlled, usually expressionless face, and his cool, steady eyes, and I didn't care to imagine how he might react, or what he might do. All I know is, something went through me that was colder even than that sensation I'd had in Standish Thornton's red room.

We started by deciding what the things were we needed to know, then tried to figure out how to go after them. We came up with this list:

1. *Where was G. between 8 and 10 Saturday night?*
2. *Did he know, and how did he know, about the Fletcher's Knoll meeting?*
3. *Did he tell Billings about it, and go with him?*
4. *How did he get hold of Standish's pistol?*
5. *What did he do with it afterwards?*
6. *How did he get home?*

We read the list over a few times, and felt profoundly discouraged. Wally slumped down in his chair and complained bitterly.

"How are we even going to find out where he was last night? Uncle Matt could do it in no time — he'd just ask Mr. Gould where he was, then check out his story. But we can't go bouncing up to him and do that!"

"We'd sure lose a good account fast," I agreed,

with my head in my hands. "Well, never mind. Let's do what we can. If we can come up with *anything*, anything at all, it might put an idea in Uncle Matt's head. . . ."

Wally reared up with a snort.

"Who's going to tell him?"

"We are. We'd have to. We'd have to do it, and take our lumps."

Wally thought a minute, then slumped down again.

"You're right." He sighed. "Well, maybe we'll be lucky and not find anything! And we *are* getting one break. We don't have to work at the Village tomorrow, so we can do some checking around right away. And I've got some ideas about where to start."

"So have I."

They turned out to be pretty much the same.

Slade and Fry had a field day with the media. There was a lot of talk about modern police methods — was that a sideswipe aimed at Uncle Matt? — when actually there was nothing new about the way the case had been handled, nothing that would have been done much differently a quarter of a century ago. And there were some interesting sidelights.

"People think of 'twenty-two-caliber pistols and rifles as popguns, but they can be lethal in the right hands," Slade explained in one interview. "But on a night as dark as that one, it took someone who knew what he was doing to put a bullet through a man's head that way, even at close range. We feel the second shot, delivered at very close range when the body was on the ground, was by way of making sure. And that one, too, was positioned just right."

He also threw in a minilecture about crime detection.

"We're pleased to have achieved so quickly what looks like a solution to this brutal crime, because murders are usually either solved quickly or they stretch out and take a *very* long time. If things drag along, and the trail grows cold, why, it gets harder and harder to nail the culprit."

Pretty fancy language, but then Slade was good at that.

We had agreed we should start our day at the Cerviks'. Strictly a fishing expedition. We knew, from having checked with Miss Mary, that Laura hadn't gone back to the office as yet. We knew they'd be glad to hear our firsthand account of what went on in the hospital, and then we could mention something about Mr. Gould and ask questions about him without seeming out of order. Maybe from Laura we could gather some idea as to what he was likely to do with his Saturday nights. An outside chance, but better than nothing.

We got the full treatment with the coffee and Danish, a terrific pecan pastry this time, and they ate up our report. Then after a while Wally went fishing.

"But what about the people at your office? I wonder how they're taking it? How about Cynthia?"

We didn't really care about Cynthia; Wally was only trying to turn the conversation in the right direction, but —

"Oh!" Both sisters sat up, quivering, and exchanged pleased glances. "Oh, of course, you wouldn't know, but someone I won't mention found out about *that* one! It seems she was expecting a visitor Saturday night, but he never showed up. When it got to be about ten o'clock she started phoning, but he didn't answer his phone, either. She was furious, of course. In the morning she started calling again, still no answer. She knew he was supposed to go to a luncheon at some friends', so finally she called up and asked to speak to him. They told her he hadn't showed up and

100

they'd been calling his home, too. Well, the up-shot of it was that after a while they decided to notify the police. The police went over to his place for a look around — and that's when they found him. Since the other people did the notifying, Cynthia's name was kept out of it, which was just as well. No sense dragging in that sort of thing, now that he's dead. It would only hurt poor Nat-alie. His wife, you know."

Here was the opening!

"I hear Mr. Gould's gone up to Maine to bring her home," I said.

"That's right, and I'm not surprised. To tell the truth, he thinks a lot more of her than Mr. Billings ever did!"

"It's lucky he wasn't off for the weekend some-where," said Wally.

"Oh, Mr. Gould isn't much of a one for gadding about, he's a real stay-at-home. As a matter of fact, yesterday morning, before all this terrible business came up, he phoned me to see how I was doing. He's *so* thoughtful! He even asked if we'd watched 'Masterpiece Theatre' Saturday night, be-cause he knew we're following the series that's on now, just as he is. We're both great fans of 'Mas-terpiece Theatre'; we've often had little chats about the stories at the office. We had quite a talk yesterday about this last one, too — he was really feeling very chatty, I must say. He's quite good about analyzing performances, and picking out the best scenes, and all that."

By now we were finding it hard to sit still and act casual. Trying not to seem as if I were having trouble with my breathing, I asked an important question.

"When is it on? Maybe we ought to watch it sometime."

"Oh, I wish you would, you'd love it! So much better than the regular junk that's on TV! This episode was a two-hour one, and it came on at — when was it, Mary?"

"Eight to ten."

"That's right, eight to ten."

Right through the time when things were happening on Fletcher's Knoll! If Mr. Gould had been sitting home watching the show, then all was well and we would owe him an apology we could never make. But on the other hand . . .

Wally stood up. He couldn't have sat still another minute. But at least he didn't make our leave-taking too abrupt.

"So you think there'll be new wedding bells before long, huh, Miss Laura?"

She responded coyly.

"Well, after a while, I shouldn't be surprised. Now that the way is clear, I don't think Natalie will have the slightest objection!"

Not long after that Wally looked at his watch and said, "Hey, Les, we'd better get going!"

10

WE HOPPED ON OUR BIKES AND
got out of sight, then stopped for a conference. It
was make-or-break time.

We were thinking along the same lines again.
There was no question about where we should go
next.

When we reached the head of Queen Anne's
Road, a squad car was straddled halfway across it,
with Officer Marty Ferman standing beside it.

"Hi, Marty! What's up?"

"Oh, the usual. All the vultures are showing
up, wanting to see the scene of the crime. We got
orders to keep everybody away. Where you going?"

"We take care of Mr. Gould's yard. We've got
some work to finish up there."

"Okay, go ahead."

We thanked him and buzzed on up the road. As we passed Thornton Farm, we wondered how Hester Thornton was making out. Witch or not, she was probably miserable and scared.

When we were near Mr. Gould's place, Wally said, "Let's hope Jessie is outside someplace where you can keep an eye on her. All I need is five minutes."

But Jessie wasn't outside, she was in her apartment over the garage. Mr. Gould's garage was a small barn, and sometime or other he'd had the upper part of it made over into living quarters, which had come in handy when he decided to hire Jessie.

When she heard us arrive, she ran up a window screen so that she could stick her head out and glare at us. She was obviously in a bad mood, even worse than usual. I wondered if it had to do with her head witch's being held as a murder suspect.

"What do *you* want?"

"We didn't quite finish the trimming last time."

"Ha! I can believe *that!* I looked things over after you left, and I never seen 'em worse!"

"We're sorry, Jessie," I said. "If you'll come out and show us the bad places, we'll get right at them."

"I'm too busy. Find 'em yourselves!" She pulled in her head, and down went the screen. But there was no way of knowing when she might be looking out, checking up on us, and she had a clear view of the back door. Trying to sneak inside under those conditions was much too risky. So now we had to make a show of looking around for something to trim while we tried to think of another ploy.

"If you ask me, we did a darn good job," Wally grumbled under his breath. "She'd find fault with the Garden of Eden!"

"She wouldn't set *foot* in the Garden of Eden!"

We went to the barn for clippers, then each picked a section of the yard to act busy in. Before long I came across a spectacular caterpillar, the likes of which I'd never seen before. Worth a try. I hurried over under Jessie's window.

"Jessie! There's a caterpillar out here that's the biggest, meanest-looking one you ever saw! Red as fire! I wish you'd come look at it, because I'll bet you'd know what it is!"

Sometimes you're lucky. Jessie came to the window again and, without opening the screen, looked down at me with grudging but obvious interest.

"Hmp! Red as fire, you say? Well . . . I'll take a look, but I ain't got all day!"

She came down and hotfooted it across the yard past Wally in her crazy skittering way to where the caterpillar and I were waiting. Behind her, Wally snuck into the house. Jessie stooped over the caterpillar.

"Well, for once you done something right. That there's a Red Dragon! A Red Dragon, and there's lots of uses for Red Dragons!"

Yuk! I hoped she wouldn't go into details about those uses, even though I was glad I'd picked a winner. She plucked the leaf it was sitting on, put both in a little bag, and tucked it into her apron pocket.

So far, so good. The only trouble was, it had not taken her long enough to deal with the Red Dragon. Not nearly long enough. I had to stall her if I could.

"Gee, that's great! I saw another one a minute ago, too, over there."

"Where?"

"Here. Right about here. Lemme see. . . ."

I scrabbled around in some leaves.

"Be careful!" snapped Jessie, and pushed me aside so brusquely I went from a squatting position to a sprawl. "Here, let me see!"

She made a careful search, then straightened up and looked disgusted.

"You probably didn't see *nothin'!*" she said, hurting my feelings, even though it was true. "Now don't bother me again, I got work to do in the kitchen!" she added, and stamped off toward the house. Wally was still in it. The situation was getting worse and worse. I knew he couldn't sneak out the front door, because Jessie kept it locked. If she found it unlocked, she'd be sure to put two and two together — she had such a suspicious mind, that one! Besides, with her sharp ears, she'd probably have heard him.

By the time she was near the house, however, the screen door opened and out came Wally.

"I'm sorry, Jessie," he said meekly. "I had to go to the bathroom."

She stopped, outraged by his presumption, and reared back scornfully.

"Huh! What's the matter with bushes?"

"Gosh, you're right. I'm sorry."

"Just you stay out of where you're not wanted, less'n you got permission!"

"Sure, Jessie."

We worked a little longer, to make it look good, but while we were at it Wally managed to tell me the news. As we'd suspected, Mr. Gould had a videocassette recorder hooked up to his television set. What's more, he had a big tape recorder setup tied into his phone line that could tape every phone call made or received in the house. Not one of those machines that tells a caller to leave a message, mind you: a tape recorder.

Jessie had not said a word about the murder, but when we stopped work we had a chance to bring up the subject. Wally called to her:

"We've finished up, so we're going to walk over to Mr. Billings's place for a look."

She popped up in the kitchen window, her eyes flashing fire.

"What you going there for? That ground is cursed, and now new wrong's been done! Standish Thornton never killed that man, but now your uncle is treating him like —"

So that was it!

"Jessie, my uncle's in the hospital. He didn't have a thing to do with this," Wally told her.

That stopped her with her mouth open. Then she blustered some more, but uncertainly.

"What do you mean? You trying to tell me he's not responsible for —"

"He had an operation Saturday, he's in no shape to take responsibility for *anything*. Lieutenant Slade is in charge of everything — including arresting Mr. Thornton."

Needless to say, Jessie didn't offer any gracious apologies for maligning Uncle Matt, but at least she simmered down.

"Um . . . Well . . . Well, then, that Lieutenant Slade will live to regret he ever done such a thing!" she burst out, getting up a new head of steam. "He'll regret it! . . . But anyway, do what you want, makes no difference to me!" she added, and turned away from the window.

What would she think, I wondered, if she knew we were doing our best to save her leader?

Although there were woods between Mr. Gould's and Billings's houses, they were nothing like as thick as the woods around Fletcher's Knoll, and an easy path ran through them. The only trouble with that was, there was sure to be someone on duty by the house, ready to keep sightseers away, and there were some sourpusses on the force who might have told us to get lost.

Another trail ran off to the right, a less conspicuous one Jessie often used when she went looking for wild stuff in the woods. We'd never had any reason to walk it, but we figured it would get us past the house without being seen and eventually put us within striking distance of the path that led straight down from Billings's house to the foot of Fletcher's Knoll. We'd heard plenty about *that* path, even seen pictures of it on TV: the path near which the body was found.

By now we were getting excited.

"He could have taped that show, then watched it after he came home, and been ready to phone Laura in the morning and talk about it," said Wally.

"And that tape recorder! We can check it out, but I'm sure you're right. It's easy to set up a system like that to record phone calls."

Wally pulled out his scratch pad with the list we'd made.

"Okay, now, let's see. 'One: Where was G. between eight and ten Saturday night?' Well, he *could* have been with Billings. 'Two: How did he know about the Fletcher's Knoll meeting?' He *could* have heard Jessie's call on the tape, the same call I heard. 'Three: Did he tell Billings about it, and go with him?' He *could* have."

"Everything's *could have*," I said. "But still . . ."

"Right. He could have come over to Billings's place early that evening and told him about the meeting — I'll bet he didn't *phone* him!"

"That's for sure! Billings probably recorded calls, too."

"Sure thing. But anyway, whether Mr. Gould suggested it or not, the idea of sneaking down there and giving Standish a shock with that bullhorn was obviously the kind of thing Billings would enjoy doing — we know that. We heard him laughing."

Wally looked at the list again.

" 'Four: How did he get hold of Standish's gun?' That's the toughest one of all."

"I've been thinking about that," I said. "He probably knew Standish kept it in his glove compartment, and left it there between sessions at the Target Club. Maybe they even gave each other rides sometimes, back in the days before Standish got so spooky — in fact, maybe they *still* did, who knows? Anyway, let's say he also knew Standish was careless about locking his car. So he and Billings sneak down the path in plenty of time, and nothing is happening. Mr. Gould says he knows how to slip over toward the Thorntons' house and see if anything's going on there. He goes over, stays out of sight, and waits till he sees the procession start out for the knoll. Then he grabs the gun, goes back, and joins Billings in time for the bullhorn performance. After that they take off for the house, and on the way . . ."

Wally gave my wild ideas their due.

"Not bad. It's like everything else — we're not sure about anything, but it's all possible. And one thing's important. He could take it step by step, without putting himself in a risky position. At any point along the line, if something didn't work out, he could drop it all then and there and be safe. If he couldn't get the pistol, for instance, he could simply go back to Billings and forget about murder — for now, at least."

"Okay, so all we can do is keep going, and hope we come up with something that's more than just *possible*."

We started along the trail.

11

IF WE HADN'T BEEN SO INTENT ON
what we were doing, we would have enjoyed that
walk. The path rambled through the woods and
into little clearings, almost meadows, sloping gently
toward the foot of Fletcher's Knoll. At one point
we passed a small pond with lots of lily pads on
it, and frogs popping into the water all along the
edge as we went by. Here and there forgotten stone
walls marked off onetime pastures that had long
since returned to woodlands. At a point where the
path leveled off and then climbed again slightly,
we came to a patch that was still a muddy bog
from rains we'd had a few days earlier. Here we
saw something that stopped us.

"Hey, look at this, Les! Somebody came through
here who wasn't watching where he was going."

114

"Or couldn't *see* where he was going."

There were several footprints in the mud, or at least they suggested footprints. They were little more than holes filled with muddy water, and so shapeless it was hard to tell whether someone had been coming or going, but they *did* look vaguely like holes made by feet. It would have been easy to step into that mess in the dark.

The path ahead was beginning to curve toward the left. If it kept on that way, it was bound to join the path from Billings's house down to the foot of the knoll.

"Let's keep going."

A few minutes later we stepped onto the path we were looking for. Straight ahead now, not far away, we could see Fletcher's Knoll, looking as grim from this side as it had from where we watched the ceremony.

"Somewhere along here is where it must have happened."

We walked down the slope. Before long we came to a trampled piece of ground you didn't have to be an Apache scout to read. Here was where the body had been found. We thought about Billings, and Mr. Gould, and how he might have said something that made Billings turn and find himself looking into a gun barrel, and we only had to glance at each other to know there was a queasy feeling in both our stomachs.

"Okay," said Wally. "If it happened here, and — and Mr. Gould was here, you can bet he took the same path home we've just been on. Let's go back that way and really *look!*"

"At what?"

"I don't know. But let's go back the way he *could* have gone, and see if we get any ideas."

The only idea we came up with was one we already had. When we reached that boggy spot, we took another close look at those holes we thought were made by someone's feet.

"If he was here, I hope he hasn't cleaned his shoes yet, Wally. And even if he did, a good lab would still be able to find traces of mud, enough to match it up."

"Sure. Only first, we need the shoes."

We walked slowly up the path, taking a good look at everything every inch of the way. For a while there were spatters of mud on the grass that could have come from the shoes of someone who had stepped into mud, but they didn't make any kind of pattern you could be sure was a footprint. Before long we were beginning to feel that all our "could be's" were never going to add up to anything at all.

Then we came to that little pond, and Wally stopped.

"What's the matter?"

"Wait a minute, Les. What if you'd just shot somebody, and you were picking your way along this path on our way home in the dark, and you had a gun you very much wanted to get rid of?"

I looked at the small pond with new eyes.

"Wow! Could be!"

I hated to use that word *could* again, but it *could be*.

"And anyone who wanted to throw a gun into that pond," Wally went on, "would step over to the edge and toss it in. He'd feel perfectly safe, because the police wouldn't even come up this way to look for the missing gun, not when they were sure to have Standish all picked out as the murderer."

I nodded.

"Let's get down on our hands and knees and take a really good look all along the edge, Wally." And maybe do a little praying while we looked.

We were at it a long time, trying to be careful, trying not to miss a single inch of that miniature waterfront. And it paid off.

"Bingo!"

Because he had thought of it, Wally had gone

first, crawling along sideways like a crab, while I did backup beside him. And now he pointed to something exciting.

There, in a soft spot almost at the water's edge, was a footprint, a gorgeous footprint of a shoe with a ripple sole.

We tried not to get too hyped up. A footprint still didn't prove anything.

"It could be anyone's, Les. Some kid who stopped to throw a pebble in the pond."

"Only why bother to step to the edge? A little kid would step close, but not one with a foot that big. He'd be our size, or larger," I said, and Wally brightened.

"That's right. You'd only step close if you were throwing something heavy, and something you wanted to make sure went in."

We stared again at the footprint as if we'd never seen one before.

"Listen, Les, we've got to cover this up to protect it till we can get one of the guys to come take a cast of it. I'll bet Eddie Soares would do it." Wally whipped out his pad and turned a page. "Meanwhile, let's make a drawing of the pattern, just in case. Got a notebook with you? Then let's both make a copy."

We were hard at it when I caught some sort of movement out of the corner of my eye. I glanced sideways.

"Oh, boy! Here comes Jessie!"

She was walking down the path carrying a basket and a trowel.

"We're sketching the pond!" whispered Wally. We both turned pages, moved back from the footprint, and switched gears, pausing only to look up and say,

"Oh, hi, Jessie!"

She gave us her usual suspicious glance.

"*Now* what are you up to?"

"We're drawing pictures of the pond."

"What do you want to do that for?"

"Just for fun. We both take art in school."

Jessie turned her gaze toward the pond.

"Can't see where it's much to look at," she said, and while we held our breath, she stepped forward. Her foot came down within an inch of the print. If she shifted it the least bit in that direction . . .

"Look!"

Wally held up his pad with a shaky hand. She turned, and her foot came away from the print as she gave his hasty sketch a critical appraisal.

"Hold it still, I can't see nothing with you

119

waving it around! . . . Hmph! *That* the best you can do?"

"Well, we really need some art paper and some charcoal, or something like that."

"Waste of time, if you ask me," she said, and took off abruptly on down the path away from the house.

It would have been nice to collapse in the grass for a few minutes to relax our nerves, but now there wasn't time. Now opportunity was knocking, loud and clear. We didn't have to talk it over more than twenty seconds. Once we had carefully covered the footprint with small branches and lots of leaves, we headed for the house as fast as we could go.

Whenever Jessie left the house, even to walk into the nearby woods, she always locked up. But we knew where a key to the back door was hidden, under the back steps.

First we took a quick look in the little pantry just inside the door to the left, where anybody with muddy shoes would be likely to leave them till he could clean them up. Nothing there.

"We'll have to find the closet where he keeps his shoes," muttered Wally. "Come on!"

By now we were both feeling enough pressure

to scare us silly. So far we had been extremely lucky. But Jessie might come back any minute. How far could we push our luck? We raced in through the house to the entryway and the bottom of the stairs that led to the second floor — and found out. At the last second, too late, I caught a glimpse through a living room window of a car in the driveway, where we couldn't have seen it from the back. And suddenly, above us at the head of the stairs, staring down at us incredulously, was Mr. Gould.

"What are you doing in this house?"

After one dumbfounded instant, he was furious; his lips were trembling, his eyes blazing. We skidded to a stop and stared up at him speechlessly. It had never *occurred* to us he might drop by the house again in the middle of a workday, as he'd done Friday. His sudden appearance was more terrifying and nightmarish than that moment in the Thorntons' red room had been. There, at least, the fury, the hatred, the contempt had not been directed at us.

"I asked you a question! What are you doing here?"

I wanted to say something, but I couldn't. I was too frightened. Suppose his nerves had already been strained, and this was the final straw? What if he went into a blind rage and couldn't control himself? He was a powerful man, a match for Standish, a man who could hurt you badly.

Wally finally found his voice, but I wouldn't have recognized it if he hadn't been right there beside me.

"Nothing, s-sir," he said. "We —"

"*Nothing?*" Mr. Gould came slowly and heavily down the stairs. "Jessie isn't here, and she always locks up when she goes out. How did you get in?"

"We know where a key is hidden."

Mr. Gould stopped three steps from the bottom. His right hand was white-knuckled on the banister rail.

"And why did you come in? What are you, a couple of sneak thieves?"

"No, sir. We were just curious."

"Curious? About what?"

"Well — er — about your electronic stuff, sir."

Wally was beginning to recover a little. Mr. Gould responded with a sort of choked-up snarl, and came down hard on this explanation.

"My *electronic* stuff? What are you talking about? Why, all I have is a television set and a record player and — a few other gadgets, and — Now, let me tell you something." His tone became flintier than ever. "I am disappointed in both of you, deeply disappointed. I don't know just what made you come in here, and I don't want to know anything more about it. It's fortunate I happened to decide to stop by the house, but — Well, this is all I needed, on a day when I have a thousand things to do! At any rate, I want you to go out there and get on your bikes while I get in my car, and I'm going to escort you off my property, and I don't want either of you ever to set foot on it again!" he said, making every word a lash across our backs. "Give me the key!"

Wally fumbled the key out of his pocket and held it out for Mr. Gould to snatch from his hand.

"Now, move!"

We walked through the house and out the back door ahead of him, and trudged over to our bikes while he locked the door. He got in his car, backed it out of the drive, and waited. We turned into the road ahead of him, and he came along right behind us, too close behind us, like a man who was having all he could do not to gun his car and smash us both into the ditches. It was a nightmare of a ride, all the way.

At the head of the road we swerved past the patrol car and Marty Ferman and turned left. Mr. Gould went straight ahead without so much as a glance in our direction.

My back muscles, which had been as tight as cables, let up a little, and I blew out some air that had been with me most of the way, but otherwise there was no improvement in the way I felt. I felt sleazy, I felt humiliated. What would Mr. Gould do now? Where did we stand? At the moment, all I could see ahead of us was a blank wall of disgrace.

I'm afraid Wally is made of sterner stuff than I am. We hadn't gone another hundred yards before he signaled for a stop. We pulled over and stared at each other silently.

Wally looked terrible. His face was drawn, his lips were blue. It wouldn't have surprised me to see him turn sideways and heave into the ditch. He was probably just too busy thinking to get around to it.

"Now, listen! How come he never said one word about telling our folks about this — or telling Uncle Matt? Why didn't he grab the phone and tell my dad or yours to get his tail over here to see what his no-good son was up to? I don't buy his act!"

In my condition, his words were a shot in the arm — but the shot didn't last. I still couldn't see what we could do about anything now, and said so. For all our investigating, we still had nothing but a lot of "could be's."

Wally's jaw set stubbornly.

"I'll tell you what we can do. We can go right back there!"

"What? What for? We can't even get in the house anymore — and the chance of those shoes being there is zero, anyway!"

"I know, I know — we can't get in on our own, and maybe you're right about the shoes. But we've got one last chance, and not much time, and we've got to go for broke."

"*What* last chance?"

"Jessie!"

"*Jessie?*"

"Why not? What have we got to lose now?"

I thought about it.

"You're right," I decided.

And back we went.

Officer Ferman was surprised to see us again, but we gave him some song-and-dance about forgetting something and went on our way.

There was no sign of Jessie at the house. We decided to walk down the path and look for her, but we had hardly crossed the yard when she appeared at the head of the path.

"Jessie! We've got to talk to you!"

"Don't bother me! I got to get these things into water."

"This is more important," said Wally, so sharply it made her break her stride. "Jessie, we don't think Standish Thornton killed Mr. Billings."

" 'Course he didn't!"

"If we could prove he didn't, would you help us?"

That stopped her. She stared hard at Wally, and couldn't hide the eagerness in her voice as she asked, "You got proof?"

"Not yet, but we might get some if you'll help us."

"Me? What can *I* do?"

Wally went for broke.

"You can let us in the house."

"In the house? Now, what on earth for?"

"We're looking for a pair of shoes."

It was as if a mask had dropped over Jessie's face — or it had turned to stone.

"Shoes?" She all but screeched the word. "You want to look for shoes in — in — Just what are you getting at?"

"The man who wore the shoes we're looking for could be the man who killed Mr. Billings."

Jessie may not have been real bright, but the implications of this statement did not take long to

dawn on her. Her normal complexion was sort of
dull gray, but now it went white. Now her whole
world was involved in what Wally was saying.

She looked ready to fly at him and scratch his
eyes out.

"You're trying to say *Mr. Gould* had something
to — to do with — Now, you get out of here
and don't come back, because when I — when
I . . ."

Wally and I held a swift eyeball conference,
and agreed on procedure. It was time for the final
effort.

"All right, Jessie," said Wally. "If you want
Mr. Thornton to go to prison, or be executed, for
something he didn't do, then that's *your* business!
If that's what you want, then *don't* help us!"

We turned and walked toward our bikes.

12

EARLY NEXT MORNING WE SAT side by side, tense and unhappy, on straight-backed chairs against the wall beside Uncle Matt's bed. He was unhappy, too, not looking forward to our coming interview any more than we were. We heard footsteps in the hallway, and knew it must be Mr. Gould, because Mr. Gould would be on time for any appointment.

It had taken some persuasion on Uncle Matt's part for him to come at all.

"Matt, I would rather not see those boys again."

"I want you to hear their side of the story," Uncle Matt had replied. "You're entitled to hear it, and they're entitled to have it heard. It won't take long."

"Well . . . very well — but I *am* very busy,

as you can imagine. There's the funeral arrangements for tomorrow, and —"

"I know, and I appreciate it."

He came into the room now, barely glancing at us, nodding to Uncle Matt, then sitting down in the armchair beside the bed.

"Well, Matt?"

"Thanks for coming. Wally, close the door. . . . I'll make this as brief as I can, Ron. Now, I don't mind telling you these boys are as nosy a pair as we have in town. I've warned them about it before. This time, I'll admit, there were extenuating circumstances. They knew I wasn't satisfied with the findings in the Billings murder, and they also knew I couldn't do anything about it, so they took it upon themselves to do some checking."

Mr. Gould's expression did not change in any way as he listened, but now his back was not touching the back of his chair.

"Starting at the place where the body was found," Uncle Matt continued, "they began to look around. They came across a couple of interesting things, but to make a long story short — you know that little pond on Billings's property, about midway between your place and Fletcher's Knoll?"

129

Mr. Gould considered this judiciously, and nodded.

"I know where you mean."

"Well, when they got there, they found a footprint that was right at the water's edge. We took a cast of that footprint, and we also dragged the pond in the direction it pointed. And we found Standish Thornton's pistol."

For the first time, Mr. Gould glanced straight at us — his eyes expressionless, way beyond my ability to read what lay behind them. He nodded to us almost admiringly.

"I see I underrated you, boys, and I apologize. But why didn't you just *tell* me you were doing some sleuthing, and maybe I could have helped?"

What do you say to a question like that? Before we had time to stop squirming around and clearing our throats, Uncle Matt rescued us.

"Maybe you could have, Ron," he agreed. "Maybe they should simply have told you they were looking for a pair of muddy shoes."

Mr. Gould's eyes went wide, and his color changed, but he remained basically unflappable. He even eased back in his chair.

"Good Lord! Do you mean to tell me *that's* why they were in my house?" He sighed. "If I'd known that, they could have had the run of the place.

They could have looked to their heart's content, and I wouldn't have blamed them — because now that I think of it, I can see how they might have decided to try me for size as the killer! Of course! Being as devoted to you as I know they are, they would probably have checked out everyone in Adamsport —"

"Not quite." Uncle Matt sat forward in his hospital bed and cut him short, looking very much his old self. "They went on up to your house, and ran into your there. But after you'd shooed them off, they had the gall to go *back* and talk to Jessie Marshall, and try to get inside your house again. At first, Jessie was indignant, even when they told her they didn't think Standish Thornton had killed Billings. But then, when they told her it was on her head if Thornton went to jail or was executed for something he didn't do, and they started to leave . . ."

I could see Jessie as vividly as if she were in the room. Watching us go, then saying, "Hold on, now! Come back here!"

"Now, as you well know, being her employer, Ron, Jessie spends every Saturday night at her sister's home — as a rule. But this time, because she was upset by events at Fletcher's Knoll, she was afraid my men might be prowling around, picking up witches, so she walked home to her own apartment above your garage, though of course you didn't know that, because you were inside watching television. Jessie was so upset she couldn't sleep, so she sat at her window, thinking about Fletcher's Knoll, and that's how she happened to see you come out to the garbage can — and stuff a paper bag into it. She noticed how you didn't simply put the bag on top of the bundles already in the can, but pushed it down underneath them. She wondered why. So in the morning, when you were gone, she took a look.

"She found the bag, and in it a perfectly good pair of canvas shoes, a pair that had a lot of wear left in them. She thought about her niece's teenage son Chad, and — Eddie?"

Eddie Soares opened the door and looked in.

"Eddie," said Uncle Matt, "will you bring in those shoes?"

I don't really know how Mr. Gould took it at first, because I couldn't bear to look at him. Even then I had the unreasonable feeling we'd betrayed him. Only when I thought hard about how ruthless he was, how ready to let Standish take the rap for the murder, was I able to shake it off. I remembered, too, how Uncle Matt had looked when we burst in on him and told him not to get mad, but that we'd been doing some checking, and we knew who'd killed Billings. A sad look came to his face as he said, "It's Ron Gould, isn't it?"

He had not just been lying there idly.

That evening Nurse Wagner allowed four of us to come see him at once, the Brenners and me. Uncle Matt glanced in our direction and sighed heavily.

"You two. I ought to thank you, but I'm too worried. I think we might as well steer you into some kind of police work, just to keep you from drifting into a life of crime."

"Well, one thing is certain, they'll never hear a word of thanks or anything else from Standish," said J.G., and for three weeks he was right. But then one day we got a call from his sister, in her best imperious voice, telling us to come out to Thornton Farm.

The hand-bell split our eardrums again, the door groaned open, and there stood the same extraordinary black ragbag as before. Hester Thornton. And behind her, to our amazement, Jessie Marshall.

"Come. Follow me," ordered Hester, and turned to lead the procession down the hall. We muttered

133

low "Hi's!" to Jessie and got some sort of grumpy mutter in reply.

What was this? I wondered. The red room again? The thronelike carved chair? The black robe? It was. There sat Standish Thornton in all his gloomy majesty. And Wally blurted out the craziest thing I ever heard.

"Hi, Mr. Thornton," he said. "You're looking well."

I gave Wally a stunned glance, but after a moment I understood. It just didn't feel the same this time. Too much else had happened. That sudden icy sensation we'd both felt last time . . . I could understand now the powers of suggestion. It wasn't there this time.

"I am nearly myself again," said Standish in a deep voice. Except for possibly being a shade thinner, I'd have said he'd made it all the way back already. "But let me get on with the matter at hand. I'm happy to say that Mrs. Marshall is staying with us now, helping out," he declared, with a courtly gesture in Jessie's direction. "Now, we know you have lost one of your lawn-mowing accounts — I suppose you could almost call it landscape gardening — and Jessie tells us you are quite capable in that area."

I'm surprised we both didn't faint on the spot.

A recommendation from Jessie Marshall! The supreme accolade! Which she hastened to qualify.

"Well, I said I've seen *worse!*" she grumbled.

"Yes, yes, Jessie — well, at any rate, my sister and I have been thinking that our lawn has gotten rather out of hand, and could use the attentions of someone like yourselves. We trust you will be able to take it on."

Here was the high point of our landscape gardening career. First of all, we were getting Jessie back, and we had been lost without having our latest Jessie story to take home. Secondly, the chance to be landscape gardeners for three-thirteenths of a coven of witches, and the challenge of doing something with that jungle out there! . . .

Things are coming along nicely. By next spring, you won't recognize it.